MEDINA

by Jullian Smallwood

ISBN #: 987-0-6929-8501-4

once upon a time when the world was a better place. A time when love and peace was the theme of one's life.
Everyone found themselves, loving and wanting to be loved. There was even some for a shy girl named Dana. Ms. Dana Medina normally walked to school with her best friend Tanya Jones.

Dana and Tanya were best friends for as long as they could remember. Most of the time on their way from school. They would stop at the grocery store. One day they decided to go to the soda shop. Which was on the opposite side corner.

Across the street from the candy store. They went into the soda shop. They sat at the booth, ordered sodas.
Tanya also ordered some fries.

The booth they were sitting in was not that far away from the Juke box. Beside the Juke box, stood a group of guys. Since, Dana did not get out the house that much. She was enjoying the new energy.

The new-found freedom. She was not worried about anything. She knew that Tanya knew a lot of people in the neighborhood. Tanya older brother was the captain of the local high school football team.

Still Dana felt a little uncomfortable. When the boys at the Juke box started to look their way. "Who's those guys staring at us?" "And they are still looking?" Dana whispered to Tanya, under her breath.

"They are not nobody!" "That's just Tony, Mike, Shawn and Steve." "There just on the basketball team," Tanya broke it down to Dana. Dana remained there quiet and shy like how she usually was. The two young ladies kicked back and enjoyed the music.

They really enjoyed themselves. So much the soda shop became their daily hang out spot after school. One day Dana and Tanya saw Dana's older sister there.

Dana's sister Mary was a first-year student in college. Dana and Tanya were juniors in high school. Dana placed the Menu to cover her face.

Hoping her sister would not notice her. But Mary already noticed her little sister. Mary and her friends walked over to the booth. To the booth where Dana and Tanya were sitting. Dana smiles at her sister. She wanted to know how did she know it was her? Her sister replied by saying, "you can't be missed."

"You're the only person that I know, who wears their ponytail like that." They came to the soda shop so much. Even the shop manager knew who they were. Ms. Baker like the two young ladies, so much. She liked the way they carried themselves.

So, when she needed the help. she offered Dana and Tanya after school jobs at the soda shop. Dana and Tanya both were extremely excited to have afterschool jobs. Dana's mom, Diane Medina, a single parent. Raising five kids on her own.

Ms. Medina was an extraordinarily strong woman. And she expects her children to be strong minded as well. She was of course, happy that Dana had gotten an afterschool job. Dana was the second eldest in her family.

Most of the time when Dana got paid. She would treat her younger siblings to many things. Things they may not had done without the extra money. Just the little things like going places. Going to the movies, outings, etc...

Her siblings were happy with the fact. After a year went by. Dana and Tanya became seniors in high school. Dana's sister Mary moved out.

She got married and had a baby boy. Dana was excited about all of that. Dana's Little brother started going to her high school.

Dana's brother and his friends from school would come by the soda shop after school. Ms. Baker the shop's owner really liked how Dana loved her job. She was overly impressed. So impressed, she promoted Dana to cashier. With the promotion came a raise also.

During that summer Dana's best friend Tanya got pregnant. She tried to work. But she started showing. Her little secret was not a secret anymore. Eventually, she had to quit. Her stomach got so big. Ms. Baker also did not want a pregnant teen working for her. She felt like it was bad for business.

Times were changing. Ms. Baker traded in the old pinball machine. For a couple of video games machines. The juke box was upgraded too. The pay phone remained there on the wall next to the juke box. One normal ordinary day at the soda shop. Dana was working at the cash register as usual.

When a man came into the shop to order a soda. He ordered a Root beer soda with a little bit of cream soda on top.

She noticed while she was making his drink. His work uniform. Also, she noticed his smile. She recalls it, a smile to die for.

After that day, every Friday, like clockwork, he came into the soda shop at a little after 12pm. Every time on that day, at that time, Dana looks out the window of the soda shop. She watches him as he gets out of his car. And watches him walk into the soda shop. Then when he looks up.

She pretends like she did not notice him. They both knew what he is about to order. Every time it is a pause, a slight stare down.

Then he orders his soda. Same all the time. Root beer with a little cream soda on top. Dana goes to the soda fountain to make his drink. She also makes sure, she put a little extra cream on top. So, it could have a cream foam on top. she noticed he really liked it.

Occasionally, Ms. Baker catches Dana doing something she told her not to do. And that is mixing the soda. After letting Dana know. Ms. Baker laughed about it because she knew

Dana really like that guy. When he leaves the soda shop. She watches him walk to his car. She then, watches him get into it. And drives off. Seeing him every time makes her day. As the school year came to an end.

Dana was getting ready to graduate. One of her guy friends from the neighborhood. One of the guys from her high school, asked her to the prom. John liked Dana ever since they were playing in the sand box together. John's mother was one of Ms. Medina's closest friends.

More like her best friend. Dana said yes! To go with him to the prom. Because she did not want to hurt his feelings.

They had a great time. A wonderful evening. Dana got accepted to a college out of state. She was happy with the offer, but she knew she could not afford it. So, she decided to go to the local community college. Days before graduation, John asked Dana to be his girlfriend.

Which was a shock to Dana. Dana told him she did not know. She will let him know, she had to think about that. Dana's sisters were laughing in the other room. As they ease drop on their sister.

Dana was by the door with John. Ms. Medina walked out of the kitchen. She saw John and Dana talking. She told John to tell his mother she said, "HI!" John's mother liked Dana a lot for her son, John. John liked her a lot too.

After a couple of days. He saw Dana again and asked her again to be his girl. John explained to Dana that he signed up for the service. Also, he will be shipped off shortly after graduation.

He let it be known, time for him now was limited. He thought if he applied a little pressure on Dana. That would make Dana give in to the pressure.

He was relying on her, to make a quick decision. A decision she was not ready to make. But the pressure did not work. She had to come clean. She let him know, he was a nice guy and everything.

Unfortunately, she was not interested in pursuing a relationship, at this point of time in her life. She knew it would make her mother's best friend upset and sad. She Just wanted to let everyone know the truth. She did not want to lead him on.

John stood there looking at the floor. As she broke it down to him. Then he looked up at her. He asked her could he at least take her out. Before he leaves. She agreed, only as friends. He agreed and then they started laughing.

Before you knew it, it was graduation day. As she walked down the aisle, she reflected on her past. She smiled and looked at the audience as she receives her high school diploma. She sat back down next to Tanya.

Tanya came back to school after having her baby. Tanya baby's god mother was Dana. After the ceremony, Dana's family, Tanya's family, and John's family went out to eat.

While they were waiting to get a table at the restaurant. They took more pictures. Everyone was happy and excited. All was happy today, but they all, really did not know what tomorrow might bring.
For the moment, the feeling, of being on top of the world. That big day came and went.

Then it was back to reality. Dana was back at the soda shop. Just like school days High school came and went. So did technology. Mostly everything was changing around the world. Including the soda shop.

In fact, the only thing that remain in the soda shop was the soda fountain. Ms. Baker had remodeled the shop. To keep up with the changing times. As everything was changing, some things stayed the same.

Like the handsome man who came to the soda shop to order his favorite soft drink. He came in and ordered his usual.

Root beer, with a little cream soda on top. One day he came into the shop with one of his friends. A co-worker of his.

As Dana was making the drinks. She overheard the men talking. She was ear hustling. Pretending not to be listening.

She heard that the man she was interested in, say that he was single and looking for someone. When she went to give him his usual drink. She gave it to him in his hands.

Then she smiled. "Thank you!", "young lady!" he said to her. She said, "Maybe, I'm not as young as you think." Then he smiled. She smiled again also.

He left with his friend. She looked out of the soda shop window. She watched him get into his car. And drive off. When destiny is involved. What is meant to be, will be.

Before you knew it. The man who always came to ask Dana for that root beer soda with a little cream soda on top. One Friday afternoon. While he was waiting for his order. Him and Dana began talking. He told her his name was Ty-Rome. But everyone called him, Ty-Bucks'

She told him her name was Dana. As the weeks passed. They begin to tell each other, more and more about themselves. She found out that he was in his early 20's. He was a moving company worker. He worked for a moving company.

The job description was he aided people who were moving from place to place. He worked on a moving truck.

She told him she was a first-year student at the local community college. He did not have to ask her where she worked. That was obvious. She was at work whenever they spoke. One thing leads to another.

Ty asked Dana for a date. She said yes! They met up. They went out. And they had a really good time. Dana had the time of her life. Dana was so happy. When she got home from her date.

Even her mother noticed how happy she was. Her mother asked her why she was so happy. Dana told her mother about her date. The main thing Dana's mother wanted to know was what type of job did he have.

Plus, how was his personality. Dana explained to her that he had a good job. And he had a great personality. And the top it all off. He likes me. Dana smiled at her mother. As they sat at the kitchen table.

After a while talking to her mother. She gave her mother a kiss on the cheek. Then she went to rest up. She was tired from her date. Weeks came and went. Dana's mother noticed she was coming home later and later.

One day Ms. Medina waited up. Cause she wanted to have a talk with Dana. When she came home. She told Dana she wanted to talk to her.

Dana told her mom that she was tired from work and school. Her mother told her she understood that. But what she wanted to say will only take a minute of her time. Dana had to say okay. You would too. If you saw the look on Ms. Medina's face. Dana and her mom sat at the kitchen table across from one another.

First, she asked her was she having sex. Dana replied by saying no not yet. Her mother was shocked by her response. The next question that was on Ms. Medina's mind. Did you ever have sex before?

Again, Dana said no, not yet. Ms. Medina looked dead into Dana's eyes as she answered the questions. Well, when you decide to, make sure you protect yourself.

Make sure he wears protection. Her moms, told her, her main concern was making sure she finishes college. She should think about her education before she thinks about sex and relationships.

Ms. Medina explained to Dana, that relationships are good for the feelings. But it can also change the dynamics of one's life. It could take you to many different paths and places in life. As they talked.

The conversation got deeper. She began to tell Dana about her life. How she fell in love with her father. How her and Dana's father was so much in love. So, they thought! Then before she knew it, she was single with six kids and no man.

Once your dad and I realized that the only thing we had in common was sex. Eventually, that was not enough for both. That is when their relationship got rocky.

Especially when it came to many mouths needed to get feed. She told her the struggle is real. Nevertheless, they stayed together until Dana's father got murdered.

Dana's father got murdered during a store robbery that went wrong. Dana asked her mother did she miss her dad. She told her of course she did.

Plus, she will always have love for the father of her children. Ms. Medina looked, into Dana's eyes and told her, she just did not want her to go down that same path.

She just wanted the best for Dana. Ms. Medina also brought up Dana's sister Mary's current relationship status. Their conversation got extremely deep.

Other times it was more like Dana being interrogated. They had an intense conversation. They sat there for hours. As Ms. Medina sipped on her cup of coffee.

Dana told her mom, that she understood, everything her mother said Dana made a mental note of it all. The next day, work as usual. Dana at the soda shop. As she opens the shop in the morning. She does what she does every morning, every day.

First, she sweeps the shop's floor. Then she mops. After she looks outside the window of the soda shop. She looks outside onto the street.

Waiting until the floor dries. Afterwards, she flips the sign on the doors to the soda shop. From closed to open. Every occasionally, she reads one of her college books.
While she waits for customers.

Some days the soda shop be busy. Other days it be slow. Every Friday Ty came into the shop to get his favorite drink. That is when Dana be smiling ear to ear. In fact, they both be smiling at one another.

When they saw one another. It was always like a magnetic force beyond explanation. A power that describes love. Everyone in the room could feel it. By this time when Dana got off work.

She spent time together at the shop. Until Ty got off work. He would pick her up. So, they can spend some time together. If she did not have any college classes for the evening, she was able spend even more time with TY. Ty would call the soda shop to speak to Dana when he did not stop.

They flowed at their own pace. When it came to their relationship/ friendship. As time to its course. Dana and Ty got closer and closer. closer than close. Eventually, attraction took over. The physical took control.

 The physical took to it a whole other new level. The desire for one of another. The feelings just could not be held. All the while they had a mutual understanding and respect for each other.

At this point of time Ty lived in a room, that he rented. Dana still lived home with her mother. Dana wanted to get a better job.

She began to search for better employment. After many applications, job interviews. The day finally came, Dana got a new and better job. When the bank job called her back for a second interview.

After the interview, she was asked when she would be able to start. She asked could she start her training at the end of the month. The manager looked puzzled. But when explained, she wanted to train her replacement at the soda shop.

The manager at the bank allowed her to do that. He liked the fact that she, cared and respected her employers. Qualities that made Dana who she was. Was a plus in any workplace.

As she prepared to leave the soda shop job behind her. Ms. Baker wished her most valued employee the best. Ms. Baker and Dana sat down, and they had a cup of soda.

After she closed the store for the night. Ms. Baker carried on about how proud she was of Dana's accomplishments. Ms. Baker told Dana, she remembered when she started her job at the soda shop as a teenager.

Now seeing her grow into a nice beautiful young woman. Dana had tears in her eyes. Dana told Ms. Baker she will be right back. she wanted to go the lady's room to wipe her face. As she was in the bathroom.

Little to her knowledge, everyone Dana knew were hiding in the stock room. This included her mother and siblings. Dana came out to everyone saying "surprised!" Dana did not know what to do nor say.

She was overwhelmed with emotions. She was totally caught off guard. Because when she came out the bathroom, the shop lights were off. Since, Ms. Baker was old in age.

Dana first figured that Ms. Baker might had forgotten that she was there. she had done that before. But that was not the case. They got her good. All she could do was to smile and blush. The night got even better, more surprises to come.

Like, when Ty came from the back with a big cake. Dana did not know what to do, at this point of time. Ty placed the gigantic cake on the soda shop counter.

After he did that. He went to place a kiss on Dana's cheek. As he went for the cheek. Dana turned her head around. His lips landed right on her lips. The people at the party stood there shocked. Dana's younger sisters made a gesture.

 Everyone heard Ms. Medina say, "Alright now!" From the back of the crowd. Dana looked at her mother. They caught eye contact.

Then Dana's mother started laughing. Dana felt relieved. Everyone had a great time. They partied the night away. At the end of the party.

Dana told Ms. Baker that she will always come by the soda shop to visit. Ms. Baker told Dana that she better! They hugged and smiled at one another.

Chapter 2

Just like time. Life goes on. Just seemed like yesterday, Dana left the soda shop. Now working at the bank. She works the neighborhood National Bank. She worked as a bank teller. Same as Ty used to visit Dana at the soda shop. Now he came to the bank Dana worked at to cash his check.

Within a couple of months. Ty opened, a bank account. With the help of Dana. Dana and Ty grew even closer. So close, eventually Dana got pregnant.

At first, Dana thought her period was off track. She thought because of her extra workload. Dealing with the stress of work and school. College finals can take a toll on anybody.

All these things can be quite stressful. Juggling school and the full-time job. She felt like she was not getting enough sleep. She knew she was not eating right. After speaking to her sister, Mary. She decided to take a pregnancy test.

The results brought a lot of mixed feelings. Also, morning sickness. For sure, one of the things that was on Dana's mind, was the fact of being prepared. Being ready. Ready to take care of a baby. Dana and Ty had plans.

Plans to wait to have a family. Wait until at least she finished college. They knew she only had another year and a half to go. Until she has her degree.

Plus, Dana still was living home with her mother and siblings. The next morning after receiving the results of the home pregnancy test. She left the house with a lot on her mind. So much on her mind. She left the box of the pregnancy test in the bathroom garbage. Which was not a highly intelligent move to make.

While Dana went on with her usual daily routine. Which consisted of working at the bank. And going to school in the evening. As usual Ms. Medina always got home before Dana.

Work and school were hard for Dana, especially that day. So much on her mind. Her thoughts were running wild. As to be expected. Her mind was not focused. She began to daydream in class.

Her professor had to wake her up at the end of class. After calling her name a couple of times. She finally responded. Then the professor asked her was she all right. Also, was his class that boring that people fall asleep in it.

She let him know that his class was not boring. She just had a lot on her mind. She apologized to him, for sleeping in class. She vowed to him, that she would not do that again. Professor Smith told her that she did not look so well. He asked her was she sick or something.

She agreed with him, maybe that was the case. Deep down inside, she knew that was not the case. At this point of time her business will remain confidential. After class she remained on campus as she waited for TY to come and pick her up. Ty arrived at the campus to pick her up like always.

 As Dana got in the car, she let it be known that they needed to talk. She had a serious look on her face. Ty had a puzzled look on his. As Ty was driving, he looked over at Dana while he stops for a red light. At first, she came off very defensive. Like she did not want to talk or be bothered.

When she did speak. She asked him what he thought about having a family. He answered by saying, he thought she already made up the plans about that. She had a serious look on her face. She really wanted his output on this.

He answered her honestly. He was not ready for a family. But he did say he was not going to stand in God's plans.

What he really was saying. Pretty much, whatever happens, happens! Dana told him she needed him to pull the car over So, they could talk. He did what she asked him to do. After he put the car in Park and took his foot off the brake. He looked directly into her eyes.

She told him to stop looking at her. He did not want any problems. He just looked the other way. Then she dropped a bomb on him. She laid down the facts to him. She let him know she was pregnant. She paused, waiting for a response. She was looking for a reaction.

First Ty looked at the floor of the car. Then a smile came to his face. While smiling he looked at her, to her amazement. He shocks her with his response. He was extremely happy with the news.

As he drove, he was telling her how excited he was. She was happy that he took the news the way he took it. She told him she made a doctor's appointment.
 She explained to him, she really did not know how many months, she was.

Ty was extra nice to Dana that evening. When they got in front of Dana's building. He walked her upstairs to her apartment. He carried her bags upstairs for her. One hand carried her book bag. His other hand-held Dana's hand.

Ty gave Dana a kiss and a great big hug. As Dana put her key in the door. She was smiling ear to ear. Only to be greeted by her mother on the other side of the door. Ms. Medina began to question Dana.

Before Dana could get a word in. Her mother had already asked her a whole bunch of questions. Which totally caught her off guard. "Dana is it something you need to tell me?" Ms. Medina said to Dana. Dana did not know what to do.

Dana just looked at her mother scared and confused. "Dana it's alright" "tell me what you have to tell me" Ms. Medina said to her daughter. Ms. Medina let Dana know what she found in the bathroom garbage. She discovered it when she was changing the bathroom garbage bag. Dana did not know what her mother was talking about.

Until her mother mentions a pregnancy box. Then Dana remembered she forgot to take out the bathroom garbage. Like she planned to. Ms. Medina stood there waiting for Dana to tell her the truth. Dana had no choice, but to tell her mother the truth.

The question that needed to be answered. Was she or was she not pregnant? Both stood there looking at each other eye to eye. Dana told her mother, yes, she was pregnant. Dana let her mother know, she really did not want her mother to find out the way she did. She apologized about that.

Ms. Medina was not mad, angry nor upset with Dana. She was a little disappointed. Ms. Medina was more concerned about Dana's life. Ms. Medina asked Dana how she knew about Ty.

Normal things mothers would ask their daughters, who was pregnant. Questions like, have she ever met his mother. His job status. How they plan to take care of a baby. Before Dana sat down with her mother.

Dana went to make her mother coffee. Ms. Medina sat at the kitchen table. Dana got water from the refrigerator. Then she sat down at the table with her mother.

She began the conversation with Ty's age. Ty was twenty-two and Dana was nineteen going on twenty. As for Ty's mother. She passed away when he was nine. TY was raised by his father. Ty had two brothers and two sisters.

With one of his brothers' being his twin? His brothers went to live with his father's parents. His sisters lived with his mother's parents. On holidays he would see his sisters. They lived closer. They lived in New Jersey.

In fact, after he turned 13years old. He lost contact with is brothers. When His grandparents moved down south. After a couple of years after the passing of his mother. His father got remarried.

Mostly all his sibling did not want to have anything to do with his father. They really did not want to have a stepmother. His stepmother and his father had two children of their own. Days he felt like he was part of the family.

Other days he felt like he was an extra burden on his father and his wife. Especially, due to the fact it was hard to gain any type of respect from his stepmother. It was not that he did not care about his stepmom. He just felt like he was second to her own children.

Of course, his father was loyal to his wife. He felt like they were just tolerating him. So, he decided after he graduated out of high school.

To get a job. He landed a good job working at a moving company. When Dana first met him, he was a helper. The owners of the company liked him so much. They helped him get the license to drive the moving truck.

Once he passed the road test. They promoted him to the driver's position. With the job promotion, he could move out on his own. Dana told her mother Ty's story. His origins.

Plus, the fact she knew Ty for years. She knew Ty even before they began to date. She explained how they met. How Ty used to come to the soda shop and order the same drink. How they began their friendship which became a relationship.

She told her mother how she felt about him from the very first time she ever laid eyes on him. She told her mother that her and her baby will be all right.

Ty was going to take care of them. In fact, she told her Ty was looking for a bigger place. Dana's mother listened to what Dana had to say. As Dana sounded like she had it all together.

Ms. Medina still was overly concerned. Just like all mothers are and will be. She let Dana know, no matter what happens. She is going to be there for her. She wanted Dana to understand what she said was all good and everything.

But she should also put herself in a position, to take care of her baby, if necessary. She was not saying. that he will not. But just in case. Dana understood where her mother was coming from. As their conversation came to an end.

Both agreed on the same conclusion. It never hurts to have a backup plan. They both just wanted her and her baby to be happy and taken care of. Dana continued to work at the bank.

Unfortunately, after the term ended. Dana decided to take a break from college. Dana went to see a doctor to see how everything was going on in her pregnancy. The doctor told her, her and her baby was doing simply fine. Ty would normally take Dana to her doctor's appointment.

Whenever he could. Other times she got a ride from her best friend Tanya. Now, Tanya's son, Dana's god son was 3 years old.

Dana was learning the way life would be with a child. She saw how things could go terribly wrong with having a baby. She saw what Tanya had to go through with her baby father.

By the time Tanya son was 1 years old; Tanya and Shawn's relationship went downhill. Beyond repair. The outcome was Tanya had to raise her son by herself. Tanya did have a new man. But she understood, and felt like, you cannot ask another man to raise a child that was not his own.

She was not saying her boyfriend would not step up when needed, or necessary. Tanya was telling Dana that her boyfriend was so good to her and her son. She wants to give him a baby of his own.

As she said that story to Dana. They looked at one another, then they started laughing. Tanya was serious though. Tanya reminded Dana that she lives with her man.

Plus, her man pays all the bills. She drives the car that he bought her. She went on to say, it would be only right to give him a child of his own.

Since, he always talked about what he would do if he had a child of his own. Still Tanya was not sure. She knew her reality was, at this point of time. That would not be a very smart move to make.

The major factor, Tanya did not want to go down the same road, as she did before. Dana was so happy with the fact of knowing she was having a baby. She was making plans for her and her baby from the moment she found out she was pregnant.

Just the fact of her being with child. Dana made sure she followed the doctor's instructions. She ate healthier. Took her vitamins. She wanted to make sure she was going to have a nice healthy baby. Ty was happy too. He got a new apartment which was bigger than what he had before.

As he moved into his new apartment. He asked Dana to move into his new place. She politely turned down his offer. Mainly due to the fact she was not ready, yet. After leaving school, she had extra time on her hands.

She decided to get her driver's license. She went to the Department of Motor Vehicles and got her driver's permit.

At first, Ty said he would teach her how to drive. But after one day of teaching(learning) how to drive. Ty and Dana came to a mutual agreement.

The agreement consisted of it would be best for her to go to a driving school. As Dana followed her game plan. She went to the 5-hour class.

After passing that. She took about ten driving lessons. With the help of her instructor. She passed on her first go around. She was happy and proud of her short-term achievement.

 So far so good. Dana was going to her doctor's appointments, like she supposed too. All was going simply fine. Dana's sister Mary and her best friend Tanya took Dana out. They went to dinner, so they could start planning for Dana's baby shower.

 The three talked and ate. Mary was glad they decided to go to an all you can eat buffet. They talked about, who is going to cook, who is finding a place where they are going to have the baby shower. That was the main thing they discussed about Dana's baby shower.

Even though Dana felt like it was too soon. But after they explained it to her, she understood, why it is best to plan early. The reason was because time flies.

After that night. Everyone knew exactly what they must do to make this event a success. When she got home, she began to get together an invitation list. A list of friends and family. A little later Ty called her on the phone. She told him what she was doing.

He asked her could he invite people. She was like, sure why not. He wanted to invite his sisters, aunts, and stepmom. First Dana paused. Because she knew deep down inside; he could not stand his stepmother. But if that is what he wants.

It shall be done. Dana was excited to be able to finally meet his sisters. She knew Ty's sisters lived in New Jersey. They barely came to New York.

Due to the fact, they really did not care for their father's wife. Still, they came out of respect for their father. They only came to New York City on things, like holidays.

Even then, they only stayed for a short period of time. So, whenever she asked Ty about them. He really could not answer any questions asked about his sisters. All he knew, he loves them, and they love him.

Like he told her before when his mother passed away when he was nine. His sisters were just about grown then. Him and his brother was the youngest in the family. When it came down to Ty's family, she left it alone. It was too complicated to her.

As time flew on through. Dana was 6 months pregnant. Dana feelings, she was great on days, she was just getting by. Dana called everyone she knew to ask them was she getting fat. She went on to tell her sister Mary, she felt like a water buffalo.

Dana complained to her mother that she was hungry all the time. MS. Medina just laughed. She told Dana what she thought, she reminded Dana that she was eating for two. Dana only could laugh too, after she thought about it. How dumb her question really was?

Dana was trying to work as much as she could possibly work. She knew she could not keep working for her whole pregnancy.

As she went into her 8 months of her pregnancy, she had to leave her job. After the doctor's orders. He even gave her a letter to give to her employer.

Explaining why she had to leave her place of employment. Dana bought her doctor's note to her job. Her job manager had a soft heart for her. He told her after she has the baby. She could come back to work. She was happy to hear about that. He always like her professionalism.

Which he always praised her about. She still had a job. That took stress off her mind. At home with her mother and her siblings. Everyone was getting bigger when it came down to her little brothers and sisters.
There were no little kids living there anymore.

With all of them living there as kids their apartment seemed so big. As they grew in age and size. The realization of how small the apartment was. Everyone had a life of their own. Her younger siblings were just being teenagers. What they were. That came with loud music and a loud television.

Yelling and screaming. Every time, Dana called herself complaining. Her mother reminded her, that nobody told her to get pregnant. Ms. Medina told Dana, so who problem was that.

Plus, that was not Ms. Medina's problem. Nor was her other kid's problem. Dana realizes every time she said something. It fell on deaf ears. Nobody cared about what she had to say, or how she felt when it came down to the pettiness outbreaks, she was offering to them. So, after months and months of Ty asking.

She finally took him up on his offer. Dana decided to move in with Ty. She knew for sure, there would not be all that noise at Ty's place. Overall, she found it to be more relaxing at Ty's place.

When she finally got all her things out of her mother's apartment. She kissed her mother and said goodbye. Her mother looked at her.

She asked her why she was talking to her like she was dying or something. Ms. Medina laughed at Dana. She knew Dana was only moving to the other side of the neighborhood. Ty helped Dana with the moving.

As Ty grab the last box. Ms. Medina let Ty know she will be visiting very soon. He was like no problem. Then Ms. Medina asked Ty when will the wedding take place. "Y'all getting marry, right?" Ms. Medina said with a serious look on her face.

Before he could answer the question her mom's, asked him. Dana answered the question for him. Dana told her mother, she was not ready for all of that, right now. She was concentrating on what was at hand, at this moment.

She explained, she had enough on her plate. Thinking about this new baby that is about to come into this world. Ms. Medina left it alone. She did not want to go back and forth with her daughter. She did not want to get into it with Dana. Ms. Medina was an incredibly wise woman.

The last thing she wanted to do at this stage of life. Was to waste time arguing with her pregnant daughter. She understood, she had to allow her daughter to live her own life. Even though she knows better.

Especially, when she remembered how she was saying the same things to her mother back in the daze.

Back then she thought she knew it all too. Dana told everyone goodbye. She gave her youngest sister, her scarf that she always liked. As they walked out the door. Her mother told her she will be seeing her next weekend.

"Your always welcome to come pay us a visit", Ms. Medina told Dana and Ty. Ty said the same to Ms. Medina. Just like she said, bright and early Saturday morning, Ms. Medina was knocking on Ty's door.

Ty was surprised, Dana was not. Like she told Ty before. Her mother was no joke. MS. Medina came into the apartment. She was checking out his apartment. She was incredibly pleased by what she saw. It became like clockwork, once a week either she went by Dana's or Dana went by her mother's place.

Especially, when her sister came over to her mothers. When that happens, they all would meet up over there. Go to the shopping area, what they called, the avenue. The ladies would get together, shop and eat.

Her baby was making sure about that. Tanya and Dana had lunch once a week. Like they always did. Plus, since Dana was home, anyway.

Dana and Tanya decided instead of Tanya taking her son to the babysitter. Dana could babysit for her. Tanya could pay his godmother, instead of paying a stranger.

Even though Dana did not want money for watching her god son. Tanya felt like it was only right since Dana was not working at this point of time. Even though Dana and Tanya knew what was going on. The public did not.

When people saw Dana out in public. The feeling people have, the assumption of people knowing what they think they know. This was an extremely cold world. And Dana was about to get a little taste of it. Even if it was unwarranted.

People just saw Dana holding a young child's hand and being pregnant. In supermarkets, stores, people only saw a young black woman with two kids. People was not afraid to show their opinion.

Even if it was wrong. As they planned it. In Dana's 8th month of her pregnancy, they had the baby shower for Dana. Dana and Tanya went to the soda shop. By then, Ms. Baker changed the soda shop to a space for rent.

They went there with the intentions of renting the place. For Dana's baby shower. When they met up with Ms. Baker. To ask her how she would charge them to use her place. Ms. Baker response to them was, they can have the spot for Dana's baby shower.

First, she asked them was they inviting her to the baby shower. They both said at the same time, of course they were. With that, she just wanted them to promise to clean up, after they were done.

Everything was going as planned. They got Ms. Medina to cook for them. Dana asked Ty, to go take her mother, to get grocery supplies from the supermarket.

Plus, she figured out, this would give time for Ty and Ms. Medina to have one-on-one time. Ms. Medina and Ty needed to gain a better understanding. A better respect for one another.

Early, that Saturday morning, the day of the baby shower Ty picked up Ms. Medina to take her food shopping.

First, he stopped at Dunkin donuts to get him and Ms. Medina coffee. Ms. Medina liked that. While they were out on their little food shopping adventure.

This was perfect timing to ask Ty what his true plans were. What he had in store for her daughter and her soon to be grandchild. Ty kept his answers short and sweet.

He kept it real! When he said his true plans was to love and cherish his woman and his new baby, that was about to come into this world.

Ms. Medina felt good to finally hear his intentions straight out of his own mouth. Because the way it was seeming to be. Dana was running the show. And Ty was her puppet.

 Ms. Medina noticed even though Ty tries to bury it with his charm. She knows he has a very raw attitude. Plus, he was a little on the immature side.

Overall, she does believe Ty was a good man. He had a good job, and love for her daughter. He had respect. Respect was the icing on the cake.

Which was exceedingly rare nowadays? Shopping went well.
They were able to pick everything up, with no problems. On
the way home. Ms. medina made sure. Before she got
dropped off.

She told Ty that it would be in his best interest to stop back
at the donuts shop. He needed to pick some more donuts
up.

she reminded him; he had a pregnant woman at home. He
thought about it. Looked at Ms. Medina, and he let her
know that she was right on the money, on that one. After
dropping Ms. Medina home with the groceries. Ty went
home to get Dana.

Since, Ms. Medina told her son to go downstairs to get the
grocery bags from the car. Ty just left after that. He did not
think to go upstairs. To his surprise, he thought Dana would
have been home.

As soon as, he got in the door. He heard the phone ringing.
He raced over to answer the phone. When he picked up the
phone.

Nobody other than Dana was on the other line. Ty was shocked. All he could do was laugh and shake his head. He already knew what that was about.

Sure enough, Dana was asking Ty to come and pick her up. She was at her mothers. He asked Dana how she got to her mothers. She said she got bored. So, she called Tanya to come pick her up.

While Ms. Medina and Ty went food shopping. Tanya picked up Dana, so they could shop for last minute decorations. She told him that she had told him what she was going to do. He replied with he must have forgot.

 Before, he could get off the phone with Dana. She asked him to bring them donuts with him. She explained to him, that a chick was starving over there. They laughed at the point. She told him to hurry up. He told her; he was on his way.

 Mary and Dana's other sisters went to the old soda shop, to clean up and decorate for the baby shower. They placed the chairs on the floor. And they were also there to receive the flowers when they were delivered.

After everything was done, they all met back up at Ms. Medina's apartment. They met back up to go over their check point list.

Mostly everything was set into place. And they planned on whatever else needed to be done. Dana and Ty reached home. Ty knew, he had to drop Dana off at her mother's at 6p.m.

After Ty dropped Dana off. He had to go pick up the cake, the rented chair that was decorated for Dana. And drop it all off at the baby shower spot.

He reached back home around 3pm. He laid down on the couch. Where he tried to get a nap in. That was his plans, Dana had another.

Once she woke up from her nap. Ty was just getting nice and comfortable laying on the couch. When she sat next to him. She was acting extremely nervous. Dana started talking about her hair do. Ty had to remind her; she got her hair done for the baby shower. Ty told her; he was trying to take a nap.

He suggested she should do the same. Back at her mother's house. Ms. Medina told everyone to go home. Get ready for their event.

She told everyone to come back in a couple of hours. Ms. Medina told her daughter to wake her up in a little while. Also, keep checking on the food in the oven. Two hours felt like a half-hour.

That is how everyone felt about it. By that time everyone was getting ready for the baby shower. Dana and Ty got prepared also. Ms. Medina began to put her finishing touches on the food. Then Ms. Medina finished getting dressed.

After Ty got dressed. Dana asked Ty to get the car washed. So, he went to the car wash. While he was doing that. Dana continued to get herself ready. By the time he got back. Dana was ready to go.

Ty and Dana were on their way to pick Ms. Medina up. And Dana's sister. Also, the food.

When they arrived. To Dana's surprise, she was amazed by how beautiful the old soda shop was looking for her baby shower. Dana, Ty, and Ms. Medina was extremely impressed.

As Dana and Ms. Medina waited for people to arrive. Ty went back to Dana's mother's house to pick up more food. Also, he had to pick up more of Dana's family. The first person to arrive at the event, was Dana's aunt Kimmie. Aunt Kimmie brought Dana's favorite dish, that she loved when she made it.

Also, she brought a bottle of champagne. While they were waiting for everyone to arrive. Dana dug into the pan of barbecue chicken that her aunt made just for her.

She ate the barbecue chicken like she did not eat for days. Her mother and aunt just looked at her. They did not judge her.

Both can relate to the feeling. Dana was eating for two. While she was dealing with that. Aunt Kimmie opened the champagne bottle. She poured her a drink. A drink for her sister.

As they sipped, they notice Dana was watching them. Aunt Kimmie got Dana a bottle of water. Dana looked at her water bottle. Then she looked at her aunt's drink. Aunt Kimmie reminded Dana that drinking, and pregnancy do not go together.

Ms. Medina told to her sister that Dana knew better. Dana went on and on about, she was not a little girl anymore. Ms. Medina broke it down, to her daughter. She told her just because she is having a baby does not define her as a woman.

Especially, a woman of color. What you do with your life. That is what defines you. Ms. Medina left Dana with that positive thought to think about. Dana sat by the window in the party hall.

Which used to be the storefront window of the soda shop. She looked stirring at the sky reminiscing on how it all got started. Dana daydreams. She had quite flashbacks. She had a revelation of the beginning of it all. The felling of it all felt like yesterday.

Tears of joy came down her cheek bone. Her mom asked her was everything okay. Dana looked at her mother and smiled, she told her mother everything was beautiful. Dana smiled and continued to look out of the window.

Ty picked up the next set of people. He went to get Dana's other sister and her niece. When he got to Mary's place. Mary and her daughter were waiting outside.

As he arrived, they just got into the car. As planned. When he arrived back at Dana's mother's place. Dameeka was not ready as usual.

After waiting outside for the family diva. He finally went upstairs to see what was going on. As he already expected. She was not ready.

Nowhere, near ready to go. He told her; he will come back for her. Or she could get a ride from her brother. She agreed. Tanya arrived with her son. When Tanya got there.

They were able to apply the finishing touches on everything. As they were doing that. One of them heard a vehicle backing up. They looked outside.

They saw it was an ambulette. They knew it had to be grand moms. Dana's brothers came outside to help get grandma out of the van.

Dana's grandmother was in a wheelchair. And she lived in a nursing home. Her grandmother was accompanied by a nurse's aide. As her aide pushed her grandmother into the baby shower.

Her grandmother was greeted with a lot of hugs and kisses. The love her grandmother received by her daughters and grandchildren. Had her aide Erica amazed. She was impressed. As her children and grandchildren came by her.

She introduced them to Erica. Ms. Smith let all her kids and grandkids know that Erica takes good care of her. She told them all to treat Erica like family. And that is exactly what they did. Treat her like family.

Now, the only thing Dana was waiting on was the music. She was waiting for Uncle Jimmy to come. He was bringing Cousin Kevin who was the deejay for the baby shower. Kevin aka DJ., Slick man.

After calling Aunt Sharon's house a couple of times. Uncle Jimmy finally arrived. Uncle Jimmy came in and took a seat. After he greeted his mother. Then Uncle Jimmy and Aunt Sharon sat down.

Dana's grandmother was overly excited she saw her son Jimmy. A family joke, Ms. Medina, and aunt Kimmie always called Uncle Jimmy; Mr. Jimmy do no wrong! Because he can do no wrong in their mother's head.

As they looked at the table, Uncle Jimmy shared with their mother. Grandma was over there, smiling ear to ear. Because her Jimmy was over there sitting at her table with her. Cousin Kevin and his cousins, Dana's brothers, went out to get the deejay equipment out of Uncle Jimmy's van.

While the group of guys were getting the equipment out of the van. Another vehicle arrived in the parking lot. As the car pulled in the parking lot.

Dana's youngest brother stirred at the car as a man got out of the car. He quickly noticed; he never saw this man in his life before.

Now the thought on his mind was to find out who was this person. He did not have to wait to find out at all. Because that man approaches him.

He asked the young man, where was the baby shower being held? Dana's brother answered the man's question with, "who are you?" "And why you wanted to know?" Then they looked at one another.

By this time, the man looked back at his car. By that time, his wife and kids got out of the car. Then he looked back at the young man.

He explained to the young man that he felt like he was a bit disrespectful. Also, he said that Ty was his son. When the man said who his son was. The young man's attitude completely changed. His respect level skyrocketed.

After the fact, not only did he tell the man where the baby shower was. He did one better. He pretty much escorted them into the baby shower.

Dana sat in an all-decorated chair. Where a bunch of gifts was piled up next to her. And more was coming. As they waited for everyone to arrive. They began to serve the people appetizers.

Ty finally came back to the baby shower. He brought his best friend Omar along with him. Omar was no stranger to anyone who was there. He was one of the friends that everyone knew. Omar went over to where the fellas were. Where Dana's brothers and cousin was.

Next to the deejay equipment. Ty made his rounds around the baby shower. After checking on Dana. He went over to greet his father, stepmother, and his little brother and sister.

He stayed over there conversating with his dad for a little while. As he talked, his eyes began to roam. He looked at the door. And to his surprise. He saw his older sisters and their children come in.

Across the room, Dana saw that Ty had a great big smile on his face. A smile of shock and happy that they came. All wrapped up in one single smile. He was shocked that they came. But he was happy that they did. Not only was he shocked. His father was also. So was his stepmother.

Ty went over to greet them. So did his father. Dana kept her eyes on them the whole time. Every time Ty looked her way. She pretended like she was not looking over there at them.

When he looked away and continued to talk to his family. She returns looking at him. Her eyes went right back on her man.

She really did not care about, anything else that was going on. Her only concern was Ty. Well, until Tanya realized what Dana was doing. She politely tapped Dana on her shoulder.

She told her that her man was not going anywhere. Also, she recommended that she regain focus. Focus on what was at hand. Also, she reminded her that the day was her day. Ty and his sisters walked around the baby shower.

He wanted to introduce them to everyone. Dana was extremely excited to finally meet his older sisters. While Dana was talking with Ty's sisters. Ty and one of his nephews, went to get the baby shower's gift from the trunk of his sister's car.

After that, they placed the gifts on the already made piled, that was found on the side of Dana's decorated baby shower chair.

As he held a brief conversation with his nephew, he could not help but notice how big and smart his nephew had gotten. He had heard about his nephew. But the last time he saw him, he was just a baby.

Now he is grown into a nice, smart, respectable Youngman. Tanya and Dana felt like everyone was there. Who needed to be there? They were ready to get started.

Until they were informed by Ms. Medina. That they could not start because Pastor Reading did not show up yet. They did not have to wait that long at all. Rev. Reading and his wife arrived. Deacon and sister Jones, and sister Jenkins came as well.

Ms. Medina Quickly ran to the back where the kitchen was. She came back with a platter of appetizers just for her pastor and his wife.

Everyone else had to go to the table where the appetizers were open for everyone. As Dana held a conversation with Tanya, someone tapped Dana on her shoulder to get her attention.

She looked back to see who it was. She sees one of her church friends she grew up around. Which was a total surprise to her. Dana was happy to see her friend. She was happy that she came. Ms. Medina went to where the deejay was. She asked her nephew for the microphone.

Ms. Medina told everyone to stand up and bow their heads and close their eyes. Then she called Rev. Reading to the microphone. So, he could pray over the food. The pastor came to the microphone. Before he started his pray. He had words, he wanted to say.

He began to talk about how Dana grew up in his church. And how God did not forget about her. Also, she needs to come back to her roots.

The church doors will always be opened to her. She just needs to come back. He looks out at everyone who was there. He told them; they are welcome to come by the church. Ms. Medina agreed.

At this point, everyone thought he was ready to pray. But no not Pastor Reading. He went on to say, that Dana should bring her baby and husband when she decides to pay them a visit.

The crowd got extremely quiet after he said that. All eyes were on Ty. He felt the unwanted pressure. His response to what was said. Was he did not have one? He just looked at the floor. Ty did say to Omar, that he thought this guy was up there just to say a pray.

Just before he was finally about to say his pray. He told Dana that he was happy for her and her husband. Of course, Someone was not minding their own business. That was the one who shouted that they were not married.

Pastor Reading responded with, "They should be!" Then he said his pray. After he put a nice size monkey wrench on this nice occasion. He sat down. Everyone clapped when he sat. Because he sat down.

Now, it was grub time. Everyone got something to eat. Overall, everyone was having a good time. But just like any event with any family.

Someone will always sneak drinks into the function. And just like all functions someone always get drunk. And do not know how to control being intoxicated.

Uncle Jimmy was that family member. In Dana's family, everyone knew it. Those who did not know was about to find out. Ty and Omar snuck a bottle of liquor in.

Occasionally, everyone came over to pour a little liquor in their drink. Simple and easy. Not for Uncle Jimmy. He kept on coming back for more. And then. He even offered to buy the next bottle.

At first, Ty and Omar declined the offer. But after they check the bottle and noticed that it was almost empty. So, they decided to take Uncle Jimmy up on his offer.

When they came back with the next bottle of liquor. Uncle Jimmy continued where he left off. Now Uncle Jimmy was feeling nice and drunk. Now he wants to socialize. Socialize with everybody. Table by table. Ty's father was tossing drinks as well. Both and few others was feeling nice.

 In the spirit of the alcohol. With all that was going on. Now it became an unforgettable monumental moment for all. Uncle Jimmy got so loose, he even offered Pastor Reading a drink. Which was out of line. Pastor Reading just politely declined the offer.

Uncle Jimmy had the nerve to ask the Pastor of the church that Ms. Medina went to. So that did not sit well with Ms. Medina. After hearing that, Ms. Medina quickly raced over to her brother.

She wanted to set the record straight with her brother. She went on to say to her brother, that he was talking to her pastor. Just like always Jimmy halfway listening to his sister.

So, he misinterpreted what she said about Rev. Reading being her pastor. For weird reason, he mistaken what he thought he heard his sister said. Before he could even think.

He screams out loudly, "My sister has no Master!" Everyone took a pause. The quietness turned into laughter. Dana's mother said, "No fool!" "Pastor!" Rev. Reading thought about it. Then he apologized on Jimmy's behalf. Everyone and everything went back to normal.

Everyone in the family knew how Uncle Jimmy acted when he had alcohol in him. That is why they told the guy who was videotaping the event. To stop the tape and continue after Uncle Jimmy finally sat down.

Unfortunately, they did not let him know in time. So, Uncle Jimmy rants were recorded. Dana's mother went over to the table where her pastor and first lady of the church sat. She stood there being very apologetic to her pastor and his wife. Ms. Medina was embarrassed about her brother's actions.

Before the Pastor could open his mouth. The pastor's wife explained to Ms. Medina that everything was all right. The Pastor agreed. In fact, they both laughed about it. They told Ms. Medina; they were not always saved.

They let Ms. Medina know that they acted just how Jimmy was acting one time or another, in their past. Before they got saved and delivered from the ways of the world of sin.

After mostly everyone finished eating. They wanted to begin their baby shower ceremony. which consisted of gifts, games, and prizes. Tanya had organized a whole list of games and prizes. This is for everyone to take part and have fun.

Many ways for everyone to enjoy themselves. Tanya started this part of the baby shower with a baby bingo game. It was just like regular bingo. With baby logos on it. Dana's aunt Kimmie won that game.

She was amazed that she won the prize. The prize of $50 was awarded after winning that game, she kept on letting everyone know that she liked that game. Uncle Jimmy told her not to spend all the money in one place. Aunt Kimmie told him not to worry. She got this. Then they both laughed.

Another game they played was, who knows the mother best? It was not, no surprise who won that game. Nobody was shocked that Ms. Medina won. Everyone had a good time with the games. They played a couple of more games. Some won prizes. Some won money.

After the games were played. Now, it was time to open the gifts. Ty stood behind all the decorated chair that Dana sat on. Ty held a big bag. So, after Dana opened the gifts, he was able to put the gifts in the bag. Tanya was the emcee for the baby shower.

 Tanya took the card off the first gift box that Dana grabbed. Before Dana opened the box. Tanya read the card. The card was from Ms. Baker. Dana's old boss when she worked at the soda shop. Ms. Baker gave her a heartfelt card. Her gift for the baby was a baby swing. The swing played music.

Dana smile and thanked Ms. Baker for the wonderful gift. Tanya wanted Dana to open another gift. So that is what she did. Dana read the next card aloud. The card she picked up was from her mom. It read, wishing you the best, love mommy.

Then Dana opened the gigantic box up. It was a baby bed. Dana looked at her mother. Ms. Medina said," Everybody needs a bed!" Everyone chuckled. Tanya let Dana know that the show had to move on.

This time Dana went for another box. That was just as big as the earlier one. Ty helped Dana lift this box up. He also helped her with unwrapping the gift.

This gift was a baby stroller. The gift was from Ty's father and stepmother. Both Ty and Dana had a big smile on their faces.

They both thanked them for the gift. The next gift was from Pastor and first lady Reading. They brought the baby a dress suit. They told Dana and Ty now they baby have a suit to visit them in church. Everyone just smiled at the gift.

Most the family and friends gave so many gifts and cards. Dana and Ty were overwhelmed with emotion. Dana had tears coming down her cheek bones. Ty was so happy; he did not know what to do. Ty bought the baby a highchair. After all the gifts were opened.

Most of the older people left. The others stayed. The deejay turned the music up. Nice tunes and they began to dance and party the night away. Soul train line, electric slide, etc.

All the latest dance moves were in full effect. Tanya asked Dana was she happy with the outcome. She told her that this was one of the happiest days of her life. Ty told Omar that the day was great. He said that he felt the love.

The love everyone had for him and Dana. Family and friends, who is what it is all about. Ty and Omar toasted to that. No drama, simply good people having a good time.

A couple of weeks later. The pictures of the event came back. Dana and Tanya picked up the pictures from the photo shop. When they got back to Dana's place. Dana and Tanya sat at the coffee table. Had a cup of coffee. Looking at the pictures from the baby shower.

Which became instant classic memories. Dana decided to create a photo family album. Just like her mother recommended that she do so. As she looked at the photos of the baby shower.

She continuously rubbed her stomach. With a great big smile on her face. The glow of her skin was a reflection, of the light inside of her. The light of new life. The happiness, the spark in her eyes.

Priceless. Every night when Ty came home from work. The first thing he did. After he washed his hands. He would go to the living room couch. Where Dana was laying at. He gave her a kiss on the forehead.

Then he would rub her stomach. He would bring out one of the blankets out of the bedroom. He would cuddle up with her.

Under the blanket. And they just watched the T.V. until the television was watching them, asleep. Mostly, everything was back to normal. Like I stated, mostly everything. After a couple of false alarms. The day finally came. Ty left for work at the same time as usual. But that day was not usual to say the least.

The day everyone was expecting on. Dana woke up with sharp pains. What she thought first was heartburn. Later, she found out she was having contractions. Dana called her mother to ask for guidance and help. She also called Tanya to come and pick them up.

She figured by the time her mother shows up. Tanya would be arriving as well. Ms. Medina told Dana she was on her way. The cab was downstairs.

Just like before. The days of the false alarms. As Ms. Medina arrived. Tanya reached at the same time also. Dana and Ms. Medina was waiting as Tanya approached them.

They both quickly got into the car. The difference this time was this was the day. As they arrived at the hospital. The pains got sharper.

While Dana had a seat, her mother went to sign her in. Tanya went to the nearest pay phone. She went to give Ty a call. She called Ty's job.

She wanted to tell him that he is having a baby. And he needs to hurry up there now. She got through to the receptionist. So, the receptionist took down the information as Tanya provided it.

She asked Tanya to tell Dana that she said congratulations after Tanya got off the phone with the receptionist. The receptionist contacted her supervisor.

She re-laid the message to him. Ty was working out in the field. The supervisor contacted the field manager. The field manager sent the message thru his assistant. Who was closer to where Ty was working?

Ty was doing a moving job across town. When the assistant manager came to the site where Ty was. He bought with him another driver to take Ty's place. When they first reached the site. The first person they saw was one of the helpers.

They asked him where, was Ty. He told them where he was.
He was upstairs getting ready to help in moving a couch. The
worker was being a little nosy. He asked why they was
looking for Ty. They told him Ty was having a baby.

Even the other worker's face lit up, with a great big smile.
They met Ty coming down the steps with a box in his hands.
As Ty walked down the stairs, he noticed his supervisor was
standing with another driver.

Ty had a puzzled look on his face. He did not know what to
expect. When he got to the bottom of the staircase. Ty
asked what was this about. He had a slight attitude when he
asked at first.

 Quickly he changed his attitude. When he heard the good
news. First, he apologized for his attitude. Then he thanked
them all. All the workers at the work site were shaking his
hand and congratulating him.

Ty got caught up in the moment in time. He forgot he
needed a ride to the office where his car was parked. As he
walked away.

And he started to look around. The assistant manager came up to him and asked him did he need a ride. They both laughed. Ty responded with of course I need a ride. Ty's supervisor drove him to his car. When he got to the office.

Again, he was overwhelmed by the love he received from his workplace. Quickly he got in his car and raced to the hospital to be by Dana's side.

When Ty arrived at the hospital. He went to the security desk. He asked the security officer where the paternity ward was. The security officer told him where it was.

The security guard told him first, he had to sign in. Ty went to the information desk. He gave Dana's name and his name. The information clerk told him what room Dana was found at.

She also gave him an identification bracelet. As Ty walked back past the security desk, he thanked the security guard for helping him.

He went to the elevators. He pressed the up arrow. He noticed when he looked up, the elevator was on the 15th floor.

He began to look for a stairwell. He found one. He went to open the door. But it was locked. So, he returned to where the elevators were. By that time, the elevator was on its way down.

Before you knew it. The elevator reached the main lobby. When he got into the elevator, he pressed the seventh-floor button. That was where the baby ward was found.

He looked for the room number. He was moving fast and did not know where he was going. Nervousness started to kick in.

Finally, he asked someone who worked there where was the room. He found the delivery room where Dana was. Well, the delivery room found him. He was running through the hospital hallways.

He raced pass the lobby. Where Ms. Medina and Tanya was sitting. Luckily, Tanya spotted him. From the corner of her eyes. Because Ty was prepared to go into every delivery room until he found Dana.

After finding Where they were. He quickly got escorted by one the nurses into the room where Dana was. As soon as he saw her. He went over to her bedside.

He held her hand. He kissed her on her forehead. Dana opened her eyes up and smiled. She asked him, was he ready. He replied, for what? She called him silly. And asked him, was he ready to be a father? He let her know, he was ready. Dana smiled again.

She expressed her love for him. She was happy that he was there. She caught another sharp pain. Ty quickly raced to get a nurse or a doctor. They came into the room to check on her. The doctor looked at the nurse. He told the nurse, Dana was ready.

She quickly set everything up. He also told Ty and Dana to get ready. After some screaming and pushing. The baby came out. New baby born in a new world. Talk about a priceless moment. A newborn, a new creation of life.

A blessing from God. After the baby came out, the doctor asked Ty did he want to cut the umbilical cord. TY looked at the doctor like he was talking in a foreign language.

The doctor cut the umbilical cord from the baby. Then the nurse wraps up the baby in a blanket. Put a cap on the baby's head. Ty was just watching. Watching everything to make sure nothing was going wrong.

 He even noticed when the nurse went back to the doctor. She told him that Dana was ready. Now, Ty was standing there confused. He asked the nurse what was about to take place. She told him the after birth. He wanted to see what that was.

The after effect had Ty totally in amazement. Shock to say the least. Dana pushed it out. Ty stood there in silence. The nurse asked Ty if he wanted a cup of water. Ty was in a trance. He did not response. The nurse had to tap him on his shoulder.

Then he snapped back into himself. Still, he had a puzzled look on his face. He did not have it all together yet. Ty went back to the waiting room, where Tanya and Ms. Medina was found.

The first thing he did, was to tell them that everything went well. Dana's mother asked him could they see the baby. He told her, the nurse said to give them a couple of minutes.

As they were talking among one another. The nurse came out to tell them the baby was in the room with Dana. Once, Ms. Medina and Tanya went inside the room.

Ty went to the nearest payphone. He went to call his father. Mr. Bridge congratulated his son. And he was on his way to the hospital with his stepmother.

Ty gave him all the necessary information. So, when they got there. They would know exactly where they were found. Ty went back upstairs, back in the room with Dana and the baby.

When he got back in the room. Ms. Medina was holding her newborn grandbaby. He asked the ladies in the room did they want something to drink.

Or something from the vending machine. Tanya went with Ty to the vending machines. Ty and Tanya came back in the room snacking on some junk food.

Ty gave Ms. Medina a cup of coffee. Which she asked him to get for her. Ty asked Dana where the baby was. Dana told him; he will be back shortly.

For now, he was in the baby ward. Ty walked to the baby ward. He was looking, stirring through the glass. Still in disbelief. That he created a new life in this world. He was extremely happy and excited.

As Ty stirred through the glass window. Looking at his son. He was greeted by his own father. Mr. Bridge also looked, into the window.

He asked TY, which one of the babies was his. Ty pointed at his baby. Both men stood there looking at the baby from the glass windows. Mr. Bridge let TY know how proud of him, he was and is.

Also, he knew that Ty's mother would have been proud as well over this great moment in Ty's life. With these words being said, caught Ty by surprise.

Words that Ty wanted to hear his whole life. To hear it now. At this point of time. Timing could not be any better. Because that hit the heart at the perfect time. That was right on the money.

Even though it was late in the game of life. Still, it was good to hear it. The nurse came into the baby's ward to get the baby. So, Ty and his father went back to the room.

Where Dana was. To their surprise, the baby was there, laying on his mommy's chest. A hospital clerk came into the room. She needed to collect some information from Ty and Dana.

She asked everybody else in the room to leave. The clerk pulled out a couple of papers, which needed to be filled out.

She explained this information will be used on the baby's birth certificate. They both decided to name, The baby Ty-Rome Medina. His first name after his father's name. His last name after his mother's name. When everyone came back into the room.

Everyone wanted to know the million-dollar question. What was the baby's name? They told them the baby's name. Some was happy and others was confused. But overall, all had respected their decision.

Shortly after, the baby could come back to the room. Everyone was so happy. First, the nurse placed baby Ty in Dana's arms. Dana was so happy.

Tears of joy came upon her shining face. She started playing with his little hands. Dana said, "Hi!" to her baby boy for the very first time.

All the women in the room. Thought it was so cute. Especially, when baby Ty smiled back. Everyone was in tears. Mr. Bridge and Ty was looking out the hospital window.

Holding their own little conversation. After Dana held the baby for a moment. She asked Ty to come to her. She wanted Ty to hold the baby.

At first, Ty was scared to hold him. So scared, he asked Dana's mother for aid on how to hold the baby. His excuse was he did not want to harm the baby.

Everyone knew he was scared to hold the baby. They all laughed at him. They all helped him out. Ty was so nervous, scared, and happy all at the same moment in time.

He quickly gave the baby back to his grandmother. Ms. Medina stood there rocking her newborn grandbaby to sleep. As soon as, Ty's father touched the baby.

The baby woke up and started crying. Ty's stepmother got the baby away from Ty's father. She held the baby. And the baby fell back to sleep.

Ty's father went downstairs to the hospital's gift shop. He came back with a photo camera. Some balloons and a variety of things he picks up from the gift shop.

Mr. Bridge took a whole lot of pictures of the baby and everyone holding the baby. He had captured the moment, for sure. A special moment that will be cherished for a lifetime. In some case beyond a lifetime. Everyone was so happy and cheerful.

A surprise to Dana, her and the baby had to spend the night in the hospital. The nurse told Ty, to make sure he keeps his hospital I.D. bracelet on. So, when he comes up to visit Dana and the baby it would not be any complications.

Also, Dana and the baby would be able to go home, the next day or the following one. Ty thanked the nurse for everything she has done for them. She told him; he was welcome. Dana's mother was sitting there like she did not understand.

 Until they told her it was normal procedures. As everyone who came to share this experience with Dana and Ty. Everyone left the hospital with a smile on their face. Tanya took Ms. Medina home. Ty's father and stepmom left. But before Ms. Medina left, she recommended that Ty go home and get some rest.

After everyone else left. Dana and Ty had a nice one on one conversation. Which consisted of them being worried about the other. They knew and agreed. That they both needed some rest. Ty kissed Dana on the forehead. Held her hand for a little while.

Then Ty went home to get some sleep. Dana falls asleep. And just like that, this day became an instant classic. Another day in history.

CHAPTER 5

AVAILABLE AT AMAZON.COM
BARNES AND NOBLE.COM
WALMART.COM

The first year of Lil Ty's life went by so fast. Within the next year, around 8 months. Lil Ty started crawling. Then in 13 months he started walking. Dana was doing dishes one late afternoon. She put Lil Ty in his walker. She wanted to keep track of him. Since she took down the kiddie gate.

Normally, Lil Ty would gain his mother's attention by giving her a certain look. If that did not work, He would just scream and cry. Or he will bump into her. He had no luck that day.

No forms of communications. Dana was in a deep conversation with Tanya. Tanya and Dana were in such a deep conversation. They were talking about this television show that came on last night. It was part 1 of a two-part series.

The way the show ended the night before. It ended in a huge cliff-hanger. Nobody thought it would end that way. Plus, they agreed the movie series was off the charts.

It was good. Everyone was talking about it. Everybody like Dana and Tanya. As Dana finished washing the dishes from the lunch, she had made herself.

She also washed out a couple of Lil Ty's bottles. She rinsed out the pots and pans she was going to cook dinner in. Ty was out making his rounds, running errands.

While she let the pots and baby bottles soak. She began to cut up some potatoes. She already had a pot on the stove, boiling water in it. Multi-tasking, still on the phone with Tanya. The funny thing about that, Tanya was doing the same thing at her place.

Same but different. Dana seasoned the chicken. Then she placed the chicken in the oven. She added some onions. Before she pushes the oven rack inside the oven. She started chopping up some greens. She placed the greens in the smaller pot.

Which she put on the back burner. All day Lil Ty just stood there looking at her. He stood there with a confused look on his face. His thought process went like this, He understand why his mommy was not looking at him.

Plus, he did not know or understood those to whom his mother was talking. Dana put the rice in the next pot. She started cutting up onions. Dana and Tanya were talking on the phone.

About everything and nothing. Dana was cutting up them onions. The onions began to bring tears to Dana's eyes. Now Lil Ty was completely confused about what was going on. The puzzled look.

He could not understand why his mommy was crying. Still, he could not get her attention. Dana left the kitchen. She went into the Livingroom.

Lil Ty just followed his mommy throughout the household. Lil Ty did not know his mother, was watching him. In the living room, Dana opened the window. Then she went back to the kitchen and did the same. She opened the kitchen window.

She got a glass of water. Went back to the living room. Sat on the living room couch. Still on the phone. Lil Ty was on her like white on rice.

Where she went, he went. Dana was doing several things at once. It made Lil Ty tired. He found a comfortable area and fell asleep. His spot was on the side of the couch.

Typical in a woman's daily routines. Especially, in a mommy's lifetime. Lil Ty tried to hang tough. But it was just too much for him. When he got back up after a noticeably short nap. Lil Ty stood there in his walker in the middle of the living room.

Blocking Dana's view of the television. Dana got up and moved him out her way. Every once, in a while, she went back in the kitchen to check on the food. She sat back on the couch, on the phone.

By this time in the day. Ty was about to come home. Dana and Lil Ty heard the keys in the door. The door in the hallway. Then the apartment keys. When The doorknob started moving. Lil Ty raced to the door. As soon as Ty opened the door.

The first person he saw was Lil Ty. After Ty rubbed Lil Ty on his head. Lil Ty went back into what he was doing before. Lil Ty went back to sitting in his walker in the middle of the living room. Ty went ahead towards the living room couch.

Where Dana was laying at. Ty bend down to kiss Dana on her lips. When Ty looked back at Lil Ty. Lil Ty was looking right at him. He was all in his face. Dana got back up. She went back in the kitchen.

This time Ty and Lil Ty followed her. Ty sat at the kitchen table. And Lil Ty sat in his walker. Lil Ty had a not so happy look on his face. Dana took the baked chicken out of the oven.

Then stirred the pots. After that she went back to the living room. Again, they followed her. She sat down. Then she asked Ty did he smell anything. He said,
yes. They were trying to figure out what was that smell.

At the same time, they both looked at Lil Ty. He had a disturbed look on his face. They knew he needed to have his diaper changed. Ty and Dana were holding a conversation.

While Dana was changing Lil Ty diaper. Lil Ty was giving his mother the side eye. Ty asked her why little man was stirring at her like that. Her response, Lil Ty was in one of his moods. Ty looked at Dana, then at Lil Ty.

He chuckled. He went into the bedroom to change his clothes. He washes up and got ready for dinner. Dana went back in the kitchen. She turned off the rest of the pots and pans. She also prepared the dinner table.

During this time Dana placed Lil Ty in his play pin. Ty came out the bedroom with his house clothes on. He sat on the couch. He grabbed the remote control. And began to flick through the channels. Ty went to get Lil Ty out of his play pen.

While Ty sat on the couch. Lil Ty sat on the floor and played with his toys that was close by. When Lil Ty reached out his arms. For his father to pick him up. Ty picked him up and placed him on his lap. He grabbed his father's hand. To motion him to place him in his walker.

Then he raced into the kitchen where his mother was. Dana was finishing fixing herself and Ty's plates of food for dinner. Dana saw Lil Ty. So, she took him out of his walker.

And placed him in his highchair. She placed a bib around the baby's neck. She called Ty into the kitchen. As Ty and Dana sat at the kitchen table. With their plates of food. Dana said a pray. Thanking God for the food. Then They said Amen. She placed a bowl of baby food on Lil Ty's highchair.

Then they all began to eat. Ty got up and went to the refrigerator to get the picture of lemonade. Before he sat down, he asked Dana what she wanted.

She wanted iced tea. He went back to the refrigerator to get the picture of iced tea out as well. Lil Ty looked at his father. He wanted something to drink too. Ty poured the drinks out. Iced tea for Dana, lemonade for himself. He placed a baby bottle of milk on the highchair for Lil Ty.

Then he sat back down and had his dinner. Just another ordinary day in the life and times, of Ty and Dana. Sunday morning came. Ty sat home and watched sports all day.

Once a month Dana would go with her mother to church, with Lil Ty. It was time to spend time with her mother and siblings. Church members she grew up with.

Anywhere and everywhere Lil Ty went he always had himself a good time. It did not make a difference to him. Dana used to ask Ty did he want to go with them to church. But he always made excuses.

So, she was not being bother with him. With that. Who wants to be? arguing on a Sunday morning. She just left him on the couch with his sweatpants on and his sports. One benefit was every Sunday Ty made breakfast. Dana liked the way Ty made breakfast. The Sundays she did not go. She will take her shower.

Put on her robe and slippers. Come to the kitchen. And be greeted with a nice, tasty breakfast. After breakfast, Dana went back to the bedroom. She would lay down and watch the television in the bed, in the bedroom.

Once a month Ty would take Lil Ty out to the park after breakfast. A place where he could run around for a little bit. Sundays was a very low-key day for them.

When the guys arrived back home. Ty walks down the street with Lil Ty holding his hand. Dana used to watch them from the kitchen window.

While she was cooking dinner. When they came through the door. Lil Ty immediate raced through the apartment to the kitchen. Where his mommy was. He looked at her and then he gave her a great big hug. Dana smiled and rubbed him on his head.

Ty noticed Lil Ty and Dana's mother son moment. When he walked past the kitchen on his way to the bathroom. He called Lil Ty a momma's boy. Dana told Ty to leave her baby alone. Then she looked down and said, "right baby?" Lil Ty just looked at her with a blank look on his face.

Ty looked at Lil Ty and then he looked at her. That is when Ty started to laugh. And continued his way to the bathroom with a silly smirk on his face. Dana was on the phone. She went on with her phone conversation.

With none other than Tanya. Lil Ty was in his walker playing with the toys that was attached to it. Whenever Dana laughed on the phone.

Lil Ty went in his room with his walker. He grabbed his toy phone. That his grandmother bought him. He laughed also. He pretended to be on the phone too. Dana told Tanya; Lil Ty was acting silly. Trying to copy her.

She liked his little routine. She told him to go to his father. Then she pointed to the bedroom. Lil Ty went to her bedroom. Ty was in the bedroom watching the ball game. He looked and stirred at the T.V. until Ty realized what was going on. He grabbed Lil Ty out of his walker.

He placed him on the bed beside him. They watched the game until Lil Ty took a nap on him. And that was that. But then Lil Ty woke up on the second half of the game. Lil Ty would not stay still.

Plus, he would not stop making noise. Ty put Lil Ty back in his walker. Lil Ty was on his way out of the bedroom. He went back to the kitchen where Dana was. Lil Ty looked like his little feelings got hurt. Dana saw the look on his face. She was not happy about it.

Not at all. She saw he was not a happy jolly baby that he normally would be. That was a concern to her. Dana went into the bedroom to confront Ty about the way Lil Ty was feeling.

She asked him about what he did to hurt Lil Ty's feelings. Ty told her; Lil Ty was okay when he left the bedroom. Dana really wanted to know why the baby was feeling like that.

A thought came across her mind. Something her mother always told her to check. Dana checked Lil Ty's gums. Maybe he is growing teeth?

 Maybe he is teething. She knew he grew a couple of teeth already. His gums were not swollen, or anything like that. She even checked his diaper. Maybe he went to the bathroom. But that was not the case. She checks his temperature. It was normal. No fever.

Finally, she gave up and asked him what was wrong with him. She turned around to stir the pot of rice.
Too her surprise, she heard someone in the background saying hello, in a little whisper. Dana turned around and looked, into the living room.

 To check to see if the television was on. The T.V. was not on. Then she heard it again. She thought probably she was hearing things in her head. Maybe it was sounds coming from outside. Just maybe, just maybe she finally went crazy.

 So, she did not pay it any mind. She told Lil Ty to get his father. Well, she pointed in the direction where his father was. Lil Ty stood up in his walker.

 He went from the kitchen through the living room into the bedroom. Where Ty was. When he got his attention. He pointed in the direction of the kitchen. By the time he got to the bedroom he was out of breath.

The funny thing about it was it really was not a long distance. But for his little legs. It was an adventure. Ty did not get up. He still was watching the game on the T.V. Lil Ty got frustrated. Ty did not like commercials.

When the commercials came on, he turns down the T.V. But when the game came back on. The T.V. went right back up. Ty was really into football. Especially, playoff season. And it was one of the playoffs games. That Ty really did not want to miss.

Ty's mind was really occupied. Lil Ty was not going to give up either. Another set of commercials came on. He turned down the T.V. again. Then he heard a word. The word was Daddy. Ty went to check the television.

He thought maybe he did not turn down the volume on the T.V. enough. When he checks, the volume was all the way down. Then he looked around. He thought that he was going crazy or something.

He heard a voice says it again. He looked down and there stood Lil Ty. Lil Ty sitting in his walker. Then looked again and turned his head in disbelief.

His first thought was that could not be coming from Lil Ty. He looked again at Lil Ty. This time Lil Ty pointed to the kitchen. Ty followed Lil Ty to the kitchen.

He allowed Lil Ty to lead the way. When they got to the kitchen. Ty asked Lil Ty was everything all right. Both Ty and Dana looked at Lil Ty. They both was looking for a response.

Unfortunately, they did not receive one. Then Ty looked at Dana and said, "He can't talk anyways!" So, they sat and ate lunch. He decided to go to the store to get the Sunday newspaper. He put some clothes on. He left after he washed the dishes.

Dana sat on the living room couch with a cup of coffee. The cup of coffee she sat on a coaster. On the coffee table. She turned on the television and watched the news.

She smelled an awkward smell. More like a stinky smell. She looked around to see and smell where this smell was coming from. The smell was coming from Lil Ty's diaper. She glances at him. And he smiles back at her.

When she went to get him. He dashes across the living room. He was not able to get extremely far. Because of his little legs.

She just scooped him up. And carried him back to the couch to change his pamper. He began to cry and everything. She noticed he filled up his diaper. Before she placed another diaper on him. She decided to give him a bath.

After his bath. She rubbed him down in baby oil. And placed a little bit of powder on him. After that he was ready for a nap. She placed at the side of the living room couch. She put a blanket over his little body. Then she got another blanket for herself.

She laid on the opposite side of the couch. She began to watch the television again. She turned to a movie. And began to watch the movie.

Ty returned from the store. Dana was about to doze off. When he came through the door. She gained a burst of energy. He first took off his jacket.

He placed his jacket on the coat rack. He tried to walk past her. Straight to the bedroom. But Dana stopped him in his tracks. She asked for the circulars that came in the newspaper. He tried to be extra quiet. He did not want to wake the baby.

Even when he went to the kitchen to get a glass of soda. He walks very lightly. He tried to do the same thing on the way back. But the way Dana was laying there. He could not help but to touch her. He began to touch her in all the right spots.

She looked at him. Then he continued to walk to the bedroom. She followed him. On her way to the bedroom, she made sure the baby was sleep and secured. She joined him in their bed.

 The aftereffects of it all. Everyone had to take a nap. Dana woke up shortly. She made her way back to the couch. Where she laid back down and continued to get some rest. Ty woke back up. He tried to watch some more sports on the T.V.

 Eventually, he felt back to sleep also. The day was easy like Sunday morning. Perfect day to relax. From morning to afternoon, all the way to the early part of the evening. As usual the first one to get up was Lil Ty. When Lil Ty got up. He went to the other side of the couch.

Where he laid on his mother's back. Dana woke up, hearing the word Hi. She looked around trying to figure that one out. She looked at Lil Ty and he just smiled at her.

Dana went into the bedroom to put on some shorts. She could wear around the house. She told Ty that Lil Ty said hi, to her. Ty gave her a look. A look of make believe. Dana wanted to convince him, that the baby spoke to her.

She let Ty know he will see, better yet, he will hear. He was on the verge of saying," yes, right!" He did not, because he did not want to hear the backlash of saying that. Especially, by then he did not know what to believe.

When it came down to this matter. A little while later, Why Ty was laying at the foot of the bed watching the game. Lil Ty came where Ty head was. And he said daddy. Just as clear as day.

Ty jumped out of the bed. Ty did not know what to do. Or how to respond to this new discovery. So, his first move was running to the living room to the couch to tell Dana about it. Lil Ty followed him into the living room.

 Ty told her the great news about what just happened. She gave him a look of disbelief. She asked him what word the baby said? he told her, he said daddy. She burst out laughing.

She told him that what he wanted to hear. Dana with a silly look on his face. She looked at him and asked, "Why couldn't he say mommy first?" Ty got confused. He did not see the relevance of her saying that.

So instead, he left it alone. During dinner that night. That is when he shocked them both. While they were eating dinner. He was sitting in his highchair. Eating his baby food. He said the word "hi!" then he smiled at them.

This time they both heard him at the same time. There was no denying that. Ty and Dana remained quiet. They were waiting to hear if he would say another word.

Whenever they looked at him. He just smiled at them. There would be no words from him that day. As the days went by. Lil Ty started talking so much.

But his words were not to the point of understanding about what he was talking. When he tries to speak, he be serious about it. Too bad to the world and his parents it just sounded like jibber jabber. The only words people could understand him saying is simple words, like eat, hi, bye and juice.

Once he learned the word juice. Juice became his favorite word in his vocabulary. It came a time when he acted like the word juice was the only word he knew how to say. He also heard the word no.

Yes, he heard and knew that word too. He did not like that word. But he learned, he had to deal with the word. Dana and Ty were so happy that Lil Ty could talk.

That became the talk of the town. They told everyone they knew. Even though he still cannot say most words. Which that will come in due time.

At least at this point of time. He could speak some words. That was a good thing. Having Lil Ty, took Dana and Ty's relationship to a whole next level.

All three of them were happy. That is all that mattered. Lil Ty was such a cool baby. Dana did not have any problems finding a babysitter.

In fact, family and friends was lining up to babysit Lil Ty. Especially, Lil Ty's aunts, Dana's sisters. They were the main ones who wanted to watch the baby.

They wanted to take Lil Ty everywhere. They came and picked him up so much. No matter what Dana had to say about it. Dana always was missing Lil Ty, her baby boy. Even if he went out for a little while. Most people who knew Dana. Knew that is how she was about hers.

Whatever it was or is, Dana always went hard with it. It felt compassion to do it. Then it would get done.
During the week Dana would baby sit Tanya's son. Her God son. Since he was her God son. She barely charged Tanya to watch him.

Tanya insisted that she wanted to pay Dana like anyone else who would of baby sat for her. Dana really did not mind; she was already home with Lil Ty. That is what she did during the week. Every week for now.

Most Saturday's Dana and Lil Ty pays her mother a visit. When she gets over there. Normally she met up with her sister Mary.

Mary also came by with her kids. When everyone reached. They all traveled to the mall together. They shop a little. They ate a little. Mainly, they window shopped. And walked around the mall. It was like they own family outing. It was more about spending time with each other.

Then anything else. Ms. Medina loved it because this was a way to keep her kids. Well, most of them were adults at the time. To keep them bonded with her and each other. She felt that way especially with her daughters.

She always was concern that if she did not do it, it would always be a possibility that the family bond could someday be broken.

Plus, she enjoyed spending time with her grandchildren. The grandkids liked spending time with grandma too. After a little walking in the mall.

Ms. Medina would take the kids to the play area in the mall. The area that was chosen for kids. Whenever she got tired of walking. She would sit down and watch the kids play.

She knew her daughters did not mind walking around the mall for hours. When it came down to Dana and her sisters. Going to the mall is a whole day experience.

Saturdays for Ty was different. First Ty goes to the barber shop. To get a fresh cut. Or a shape up.

Ty always like to keep his hair neat. He met up with Omar at the shop. Their man day began at the shop. Tanya came to the mall a little late. To meet up with them. First Tanya had to work. She worked on Saturdays.

When she got off. Then she goes to the mall. Her son was already with Dana anyway. From when she dropped him off earlier. On her way to work.

The main reason she did that for her best friend and her son was because shortly after Tanya gave birth to her son. Her son's father just upped and left her. To take care of her and her baby alone.

Dana knew that was an indirect circumstance that she had to deal with. She had to raise her son by herself. Her son really liked and cared about Lil Ty. And Lil Ty cared about and liked Markie. He looks up to him. The two little boys were tight.

Even though Lil Ty was just turning two and Markie was about to be five. When they came around one another. The two of them always seemed to always have a good time. Everyday being around one another was great for them both.

While they were at the mall. Tanya met up with them. To hangout and pick up her son. Once a month Markie would stay with Ty. Markie would go to the barber shop with Ty. Ty would take him early in the morning, to get his haircut. Depending on what Dana and they were doing.

After Markie got his haircut. Ty would drop him off by the mall. Where Dana was. Both Dana and Ty had Tanya's back. They consider her to be extended family.

With Lil Ty, Tanya's son, her sister Mary's two kids. They had a nice small number of kids with them at the mall. After they left the mall.

Most of the time, Ms. Medina would offer to watch the kids if they had any plans to go out. Ms. Medina knew it was hard being a mommy. She understood that sometimes mommy's need breaks too.

Remember Ms. Medina was a single parent in the struggle. Raising her children. She told the young ladies, to go out and have a good time. Have some fun. She told them to take advantage of their youth. Ms. Medina's motto was your only young once.

Live and enjoy life. So, that is how you can grow old with no regrets. Plus, if the ladies came back from hanging out late. Ms. Medina would have the kids spend the night over by her.

Before they went for the evening, everyone had to go home and get ready. Put a clothing bag together for the kids. Church clothing for the next day. They knew and Ms. Medina made it clear if they did not pick up their children by a certain time.

They would pick their kids up from church. Because that's where Ms. Medina was going to be. She was not trying to be late for church for no one.

That was the rules for hanging on a Saturday night. Everyone understood. There will be no problems, and nobody will not start none either. When Dana got home from the mall. She would see Ty with a nice, neat haircut.

After she discussed what her plans were for the night. She would struggle to braid Lil Ty's hair. And get ready at the same time. Ty just looks at her and shakes his head. Dana really did not like braiding his hair like that. Lil Ty did not like it either.

Especially the pain that came with it. While she did it. All Lil Ty would do was cry. The question that Ty kept on asking Dana. Was why do you insist on putting yourself and the baby through something you and the baby do not like? Same answer all the time. He is not ready for a haircut. When she says that.

Ty leaves the room. And leaves the conversation as well. Ty really did not want to be around Lil Ty crying and Dana mad and frustrated over doing his hair. Lil Ty crying. Lil Ty was not staying still. Before you knew it, she done popped the boy to make him stay still. It was just not a good look to watch.

While it unfolds. After she finishes. She goes and take a shower. Lil Ty looking at his father, like you allow this to happen to me. Ty tried not to catch eye contact with him. And if he did. He would go in the kitchen and get Lil Ty some juice. Then things became better for Lil Ty.

Depending on how Lil Ty felt afterwards would decide if or not he would spend the night by grandma. With the other kids. If Lil Ty fell asleep while Dana was in the shower or getting ready.

Ty would just tell Dana that it is best for Lil Ty to just stay home. Ty knew it was especially important for Dana to have some fun. If that made her happy. Then he was happy with that. If she wanted to go out, occasionally. He had no problems with that.

Plus, she does not complaint when he goes out with his boys. When Ty went out with his friends. It was basic, drink, smoke, and bullshit. Nothing heavy, nothing serious.

So, he could stay home at any given time. Lil Ty wanted to stay home. Ty did not have any problems with that. Hanging out all late. Late night for Dana, her sisters and friends were not that serious either.

Make no mistakes about it. They had more fun than the people. When they went out. Someone out of their crew always had some type of a game plan.

Some type of event, new restaurant or a get together. They be having so much fun. They almost felt guilty about it. Yes, almost! Because that feeling of guilt left the thought process quickly. And never returned.

Now, one thing the people had in common. Was that drunken friend. The one who seem like they needed that extra drink. And that extra drink took them out. The difference between the ladies and guys was the guys would still invite that friend out.

With the ladies after a couple times of that. They just would not invite that person anymore. Do not get me wrong they would spend time together with their friend. They would just pick the events that they felt was more suitable for her.

They cared about their image. Some lady's nights were consisted of everyone coming over to each other's place. Whoever were doing the hosting bought the bottle of wine. Someone supplied the pack of cards for spades. Or pity pat. The main thing was to hang out and gossip.

Sometimes Ms. Medina herself would join the group of women. When they plan a casino trip. Or when it was a shopping spree involved. She would not go that often with them. She let them do their own thing. Dana, her sisters, and friends always had a marvelous time. They had such good times.

When Dana got home. She told Ty all about the fun they had. All he said was next time she and her friends plan something he would like to go.

He acknowledged that the ladies were having more fun than the guys. He kept it real on that note. Then they both started laughing.

After Dana told him he would not like what the girls are doing. He agreed with probably so. Dana knew Ty would not want to hang out with a group of women. After the conversation with Ty about her night. She went to check on Lil Ty.

When she came in their bedroom. He was already sleep. She just kissed him on the head. And tucked him in. In his little bed next to theirs. Even though Lil Ty has his own room. He will play in his room. He only played in his room sometimes.

Only when Markie was there. The truth of the matter, Lil Ty was not ready to sleep in his own room yet. The reason Ty bought a bed for Lil Ty. He wanted to make sure Lil Ty gets used to being in a bed by himself.

Lil Ty sleeping in the bed with them. Was not a good look on many levels. Ty's father Mr. Bridge told him that. That is how you get the baby out of your bed. The next move is to get the baby out of the bedroom. If you left it up to the mother.

Especially with her first child. You will have a kid sleeping in your bed at 7 years old. Or sleeping in your bedroom at that age. So, the little bed was especially important.

Before Dana and Ty went to bed. Someway, somehow Lil Ty would wind up in their bed by morning time. But now with the little bed of his own. When Lil Ty sees his parents go to bed in their bed. He goes straight to his bed with no problems.

Ty thanked his father for the idea. Just a moment ago, Dana and Ty could not wait until Lil Ty could talk. Now they cannot shut him up. When he would not shut up.

Ty would try to bribe him. He would try with a new toy or some juice. Things of that nature. That is how Ty went about things when Dana was not home.

That is how he dealt with Lil Ty's misbehavior. On the other hand, when it was up to Dana, things got handle differently.

When Dana was home, and Lil Ty was acting up. She would just tell him to shut up. If that did not work, she would pop him on his little behind. Mommy justice would prevail. Lil Ty knew mommy did not play that. Mommy did not play them type of games.

Lil Ty learned from experience, what and what not to do on his moms watch. He remembered all but so well what happened to him when his mother was on the phone that time. He remembered the outcome. He knew what happened. The time she told him to be quiet.

While she was on an important phone call. And he did not. He knew he had made a big mistake. After his mommy told him to be quiet. But he kept on going. Before he could think of his wrongful actions. He got popped.

After that situation, he learned and understood how and when to read his mommy's facial expressions. That saved him a lot of time and trouble. Not to mention a sore behind. One way or another, like all kids would have to learn. What mommy says, goes...

Chapter 6

Mr. William B. Bridge, father of seven. Three girls and four boys. Five with his first wife, who unfortunately passed away. The family was not only heartbroken. Due to the fact of the nature. They also were broken up. After Lesha died, Ty's biological mother.

His oldest sister was grown enough to live on her own. She took in his other sister that was just about grown also. His grandparents took in his other brothers. His father's parents.

Ty was left to be raised by his father. The reason for the family split. Was because mentally and physically they knew William could not hold a family together by himself. Not for the lack of trying. With William just losing his wife, the mother of his children.

Mr. And Mrs., Bridge just wanted to help their son and their grandchildren. Help him take care of his children after such a tragedy. Ty and his father experienced good days and bad days. Ups and downs.

Was it easy for them? No but life was not easy to begin with. It was a bunch of times and days Ty missed his mother being around. Just like it was many times and days Mr. Bridge missed his deceased wife.

Plus, his other kids. To gain comfort, He explained to Ty, that his mother has not left them. Maybe in the physical. But not in the heart and spiritual.

To make it simple, he told Ty his mother was watching over them. All of them, all day, every day. Mr. Bridge and Ty sat down and express their feelings about it all.

Mr. bridge let Ty know, he knew it is going to be hard. But he had faith, that together they would make it. They will be all right.

Brighter days are to come. He told his son Ty, that he must believe. Mr. Bridge's philosophy was that everything happens for a reason. It is all in God's plans.

 Whom was he to question God? Who was he to judge, God's moves when it comes to our lives? He told Ty, they have jobs to do.

Ty goes to school. And he must work. Mr. Willie Bee would joke around with Ty by saying, "I might not cook," "like my wife"," Your mother!" "But he's going to make sure they eat."

He used to say that a lot with a chuckle behind that statement. Some days the food was good. Some days the food was just terrible.

Many days Mr. Bridge would place the food on his and Ty's plates. They both would look at the food. Then look at one another. Those days Mr. Willie Bee told Ty to get his jacket. Because they were going to get some take-out for dinner.

As time went by, Mr. Willie Bee got better at cooking. Ty and his father began a special bond. A bond that could not easily be broken. Ty and his father became closer. Not only were their father and son. But they became friends. Whatever Ty needed. Mr. Bridge was there to provide.

Not only in monetary support. But also, mental, and physical support. If Ty needed someone to talk too. His father was there with a listening ear. Time and a listening ear are vital to the upbringing of a young person's life. Their lively hood.

The growing process of life. These are the days that may not mean a lot today. But means everything tomorrow. In the future. Ty felt like, even though he lost his mother. His father made his world a whole lot better.

Mr. Willie made sure; Ty had someone on his side. In his corner. That he was not in this life alone. Childhood for Ty was just like any kid that had to deal with these sorts of circumstances.

Especially, when you are young, and you see all your friends being embraced by their mothers. The realization of not having one anymore. You cannot help but feel some type of way about it.

Hurt feelings, no matter what anybody is says. That is a void that is almost impossible to ever be re-filled again in one's life.

Which is even tougher, when? You are young, not even a teenager yet. That is the sad part of it all. Still life must go on. No matter what cards was dealt to you.

Days turned into months. And months turned into years. When Ty was 10 years old. His father and he began to go to church. At church is where he was able to find new friends and activities.

At first Ty did not want to go. But eventually, he looked forward to going. To Mr. Bridge he felt like that is what him and his son needed in their lives.

Not only did Ty gain something out of the church experience. Mr. Bridge also gained a lot as well. It changed his life. In many ways than he even expected it to. For Mr. Bridge it changed the way he dressed. The way he acted. His approach on decision making on his life's choices.

Even the way he kept up on his appearances. Grooming himself, haircuts, shaving, etc. He made sure he was, and Ty stayed clean and neat. Everyone took notice. Even Mr. Bridge's job. He received a promotion. Not only in the workplace. Many women in the church took noticed also.

One lady was always interested in Mr. Bridge. Her name was Jamie. Jamie Davis to be exact. Jamie had a son of her own. She was a single mom. Raising a son by herself. Her son was a couple of years older than Ty.

Ty and her son hit it off at once. They became cool. Whenever she planned something for her son. She invited Ty to come along. Also Mr. Willie if he was not busy.

Even when she put her son in a football little league. She recommended that Mr. Bridge do that as well. Which he did. All of that was making Ty and Mr. Bridge happy, beyond words.

Then it came a time when she asked Mr. Bridge out to dinner. She knew by speaking to him, that he had really loved his wife.

And it broke his heart when she died. That he remained faithful to her. Even though she was not with us anymore. The fact, that he was raising is son by himself. She really admired that about him. Clearly at this stage, she wanted more than friendship with this man.

She felt like she can offer what he needs and what he deserves to have. She wanted him to love again. That was her goal. That she set for herself. As they began to go out sometimes. He explained to her that it was hard being single and being a widower.

Raising a child in this world alone. He knew he had to keep it together. Not only for Ty but for all his children. There was no rush between the two of them. What Jamie did, was all the little things that needed to be done.

She made sure every Sunday after church, Ty and Mr. Bridge had a nice home cooked meal to take home with them. As their friendship grew so did the love, they had for one another.

Jamie would watch over Ty some Saturdays. To give Mr. Bridge a break. She will take the boys out to the movies and dinner afterwards.

 Ty spends the night over by her place. Ty really enjoyed that. On the other side of the coin, Mr. Bridge would take the boys to football practice. The more Mr. Bridge and Ms. Davis spend around one another, The more they grew as a couple.

 The more Mr. Willie started feeling good inside. Feelings he has not felt in years. He began to feel like he could love again. And can accept and receive love again. To let go. Not to forget, but to live and love again. That is important in everyone's life.

 Ms. Jamie was very patient with the process.
She knew what and who she wanted. During one of their conversations. She told him that at this stage, his deceased wife would want him to be happy.

At first, he did not understand, nor did he want to. In an afterthought, he clearly knew exactly what she meant by her statement.

It made him even more attracted to her. It made him open his eyes up, mind, heart, and soul. Long and behold, the day came.

The day Mr. Bridge came home with a question for Ty. The question he asked his son was, what did he think about Ms. Jamie becoming his stepmother. He sat Ty down and explained to him the basics.

First and foremost, Ms. Jamie would never take the place of Ty's mother. He made that clear to Ty. On another note, he told Ty that he needed someone, that they needed someone to try to fill that void. Ty took all what his father was saying to him in.

As his father looked directly into his eyes. He felt the sincerity in his father's voice and conversation. We need to at least try it out. He told his son that this will not be a negative. But a positive in their lives.

Ty remained there speechless. Mr. Willie left Ty's bedroom after the deep one on one conversation. Not before he told his son to get some sleep.

The following weekend, Mr. Bridge got on one knee and asked Ms. Jamie for her hand in marriage. She said yes! Then she said, "about time." They laughed after that was said. The smiles on their faces were priceless.

So many memories. Not enough space for Ty's brain. These was thoughts and reflections on his father and himself on the come up. As Ty continued to reminisce about it all. Like when the wedding day came. After they said I do! Things got therefore on.

 The fact that she was going to be in their lives for real, for real. In many cases, forever. At first Ty felt like Ms. Jamie was trying too hard. To gain his liking. Trying to be his mother, things of that nature. He lost it when she tried to punish him.

Also, he did not like the fact that his father went along with it. Ty felt a certain way about it. The question kept on popping in his head. Out of all his children. Why did he choose him to stay with him?

He thought at first it was to pick on him. To torture him. A few years later, as Ty was in his teens. When Mr. Bridge and Ms. Jamie began to have children of their own.

By that time, Ms. Jamie's son from another marriage was gone out the house. He was in college out of state. Ty began to feel like the way she treated her kids that she had, the way she treated him.

With all the things that was running through his mind. He felt at times, like he was an extra wheel to a car. A spare tire. Ty's little brother and sister look up to their older brother. Too bad he did not notice it, at first. Because most of the time Ty was wrapped up in his own feelings. And thoughts about himself.

Instead of playing a better part in everything. He chose to go against the grain. Being sour about everything.
So, with that, being said. He always found his self in all sorts of trouble.

With all sorts of problems. Always on punishment. Not realizing that all his little brother and sister wanted to do, was to love him. All these thoughts raced through Ty's memory banks.

Even when he dreamed, he thought about his growing pains.
Ty went to work as usual. When he came home from work.
Just like always when he opened the door, Lil Ty was
standing there like he was waiting on him. Dana sitting on
the couch comfortably, pretending like she was not waiting
on his arrival too.

As he took off his coat and place it on the coat rack. Lil Ty
put his hand out. He wanted his father to give him a five.
(Hand gesture) Then he looked at the couch, he noticed that
Dana had tears in her eyes. He raced over to her to ask her
what was wrong.

Why she was crying for. What has happened while he was at
work. She told Ty, she needed to tell him something.

First, she recommends that he have a seat. They went to the
kitchen. Ty sat down wanting to hear what was going on.
She asked him did he want something to drink. He told her
no.

Then she got another kitchen chair and placed right beside
his chair. She sat down next to him and held his hand. She
looked at him and told him, the information she had to tell
him.

She had gotten the news earlier in the day. But she chose to tell him this when he got home from work. Ty sat there eager to hear what she had to say to him. She told him that Mr. Bridge had passed away. His father. As she cried as she told him the sad news. Ty looked at the juice box that was on the kitchen table.

Then he looked at Lil Ty. He asked Lil Ty did he want some juice. Lil Ty said yes. So, Ty went to the dish rack. He got one of Lil Ty's little sippy cups. Pour him out some juice. He gave it to him. Then he rubs his hand on his head.

Just like how his dad used to do to him. Ty was in serious denial. Total disbelief. He told Dana that he was thinking about his father all day and night for the last couple of days. The feeling was so strong.

He was planning to go over to his dads, to thank him for all he has done for him. To thank him for what he did not understand before.

That now he understood. What this great man, role model that he had in his father. Tears started to run down Ty's face.

Dana went to get him some tissue for him. Ty felt bad. When he thought about how he acted as a youngster. He acknowledged the fact, that all his dad ever wanted for him, was what was best for him.

That is what was killing him inside. Dana gave Ty a hug. And rubbed his back. As the tears ran rapidly down his cheeks. Lil Ty hugged Ty on his leg. Ty felt the love from Dana and Lil Ty. Ty sat down and talked about his father. Dana knew some of the things, the stories.

Things, that Ty talked about. Things like he was always there for him. The fact, that his father believed in him. Even when he did not believe in his own self. Ty was explaining to Dana that him and his father was making plans to see his grandfather.

The plans were to go down south and visit Ty's grandparents. They already had decided for the trip. They were going to drive down there. So, Lil Ty could meet his great grandparents.

Mr. Willie Bee always ends making plans with, "If God's willing!" Because he always used to tell Ty, that nobody's promise tomorrow. Ty used to laugh about that. Looking from Ty's perspective now.

He came to the realization. That life was like that. He was thinking and talking about how he tried his best to raise him despite the fact, that he raised him without a mother.

For the most part, his father was the only parent that he ever known. Because he barely knew his mother. Now the only parent he had left, left this world on that day.

Once Ty got it together for the most part. He asked Dana how his stepmother was holding up. She told him; Ms. Jamie was doing as well as expective for this sad moment.

She told Ty. Ms. Jamie was the one who call her with the news. Dana informed Ty that Ms. Jamie was overly concerned about how he was going to take this.

Even Ms. Jamie let Dana know that she met Ty and his father at the same time back then. Dana was learning a whole lot about what was going on. And how everyone felt about Mr. Bridge. How he touched so many lives for the better.

She knew Mr. Bridge was a nice man and all. But she did not have a clue about what she was hearing about him. Dana went back into the kitchen. She prepared a plate of food for Ty.

She called Ty back in the kitchen to have something to eat. At first, Ty told her that he was not hungry. But after a little persuading. He sat down and ate his meal. Dana thought process on what was going on. Was Ty needed something to eat. How could he think properly on an empty stomach?

After eating dinner, Ty call Ms. Jamie, they had a nice conversation. He learned the fact that Ms. Jamie did not have the money to bury his father. She told him that his grandparents were taking care of it all. His father's body was being shipped down south.

North Carolina is where the funeral and burial will be. Ty asked her did she need any help getting down there. She was very honest. She had a little bit of money. Not enough for the trip. Ty let his stepmother know, Dana would be dropping off the money to her tomorrow for the trip.

After Dana dropped him off to work in the morning. He also asked about his little brother and sister, Betty and Stuy. She told him Betty was taking it okay. His little brother Stuyvesant was not so okay. He was very heartbroken.

But they will be all right. Ms. Jamie wanted to know was Ty holding up in this difficult time. Ty told her; he will be fine. They got off the phone. He went into the bedroom to get some house clothes to put on after he takes his shower.

While in the shower, that is when it hit him like a ton of bricks. He began to let it all out. He was extremely hurt over the passing of his father. He also knew he had to be strong about it. Strong for everyone else in the family.

Before he left the bathroom, he made sure he got his thoughts together. As he laid in the bed that night. He remained there for a little while with his eyes opened wide. Dana turned his way in their bed. He told Dana; he did not remember ever going down south like that.

Maybe in his lifetime, maybe once or twice. He said his brothers lived down south. That is where they went to live after the passing of their mother. Ty used to go with his father to the post office. His father was always sending money and packages down south.

Whenever he asked his father about going down south. He always replied, he had to work. He could not take the time off. As a child Ty could not understand. But as a man he understood where his father was coming from.

Mr. Bridge had to take care of multiple households. The ones where his children lived. He would tell Ty they will get down south, one day. If God is willing. The next day Everyone from Ty's job, his childhood friends, neighbors, friends from all walks of life.

Came by to send their condolences, support, and love. That made him feel good. He truly felt the love. That people really cared. The love was out there. Ty was going to drive out there at first.

But after Dana and Ty, discussed it. They came with the conclusion, that Lil Ty was just too young to make the trip.

Dana was down with whatever Ty wanted to do. When Ty got home from work. He made up his plans. He told her them. And she was okay with it. The next day Dana booked a flight to North Carolina for the weekend. After she dropped off the money to Ty's stepmom.

During what she was doing. Dana began to feel a bit woozy. She took it like it was nothing. She probably needed something to eat. She stopped and made sure she got herself and Lil Ty something to eat.
Dana felt like if she did not feel any better. She will go to the doctor by the weekend.

Dana was serious about her health. She did not play around when it came to that. Lil Ty knew his grandfather as much as any 4-year-old. Ty was happy that at least Lil Ty and his father had some time together. He wished it would have been longer. But he was grateful for the time they spent together.

At least Lil Ty somewhat knew this great man, his grandfather. Lil Ty used to call him, pop-pop. Mr. Willie loved that. Mr. Willie thought the world of Lil Ty. Ty really did not know how to explain it to his son. That he was not going to see pop-pop no more. As the week came to a closing.

Ty's stepmother left for south on Thursday. Dana booked Ty's flight for Friday night. During the whole flight Ty was nervous about seeing his siblings that he had not seen in years. Not so much his sisters. He saw his sisters more often. But his brothers that was another story.

The last time he saw his brothers he was 15 years old. In his head, he felt like time flew. He had mixed feelings about the whole ordeal. His oldest brother Ralph picked him up from the airport. Ralph met Ty at the airport.

He had his wife and two kids with him. Ralph Jr. was twelve and Annie was eight. Ralph's wife was amazed how much Ty and Ralph looked alike.

The whole ride she kept on telling the facts. Ralph reminded her that they are brothers. Ralph also told her they have another brother that looks even more like Ty.

Ralph asked Ty where he was staying at during his time down there. Ty told him; he did not know yet. Ty brought enough money for a hotel room for a couple of days.

Just in case. Ralph told his younger brother that his money is no good there. Ralph let Ty know his instructions for now, was to pick him up and take him to their grandparent's house. And that is what he was going to do. They both laughed about that.

Ty's grandparents were looking forward to seeing him. Ty liked the fact, his grandparents accepted him with open arms. Ty finally found out how cool his grandfather really was.

 As he walked through the house towards out back to the patio. Where there was a couple of benches. His grandfather words were refreshing to Ty. Things will be all right. The two of them sat outback there talking about an abundance of things.

 Ralph came to the back as well. He wanted to know what Ty was doing for the night. He told his brother that he was going to stay by their grandparent's place. Ralph wanted to spend some time with Ty before he left.

Ty agreed with that. While they were talking Ty's, grandmother came outside and asked him for some sugar. He gave his grandmother a kiss on her cheek. She asked the men did they want something to drink.

Ty's grandfather said "no." Ty said," yes, please." His grandmother went inside to get Ty something to drink. That night while his grandfather was showing Ty the guess room. His sister called the house.

She told their grandmother that they all arrived in North Carolina safely. They left a message to Ty and their grandparents. They wanted everyone to get together to have breakfast in the morning.

Ty's grandmother told her granddaughters that breakfast will be at her house. And she told them the time to be there. Nobody could disagree with grandma. The next morning was great everyone got to see one another. Just about everyone was there.

Except, Jerome Ty's brother was flying in, in a little bit. Jerome was overseas, he was in the military. It was like a family reunion, unfortunately under sad circumstances.

Ty felt great seeing and being around family. Exceedingly rare did he have opportunities to see that. The funeral was great. His cousin gave the Eulogy over it.

He was the one who gave the sermon. He acknowledges the greatness that his uncle showed to everyone. He said when his mother, Ty's aunt did not have any money for back-to-school shopping and supplies. His uncle Willie stepped up to the plate. He sends us the money.

His cousin Rev. Bridge was telling a story on how he effected their lives. Ty sat there amazed with what he was hearing. Many people talked about all the acts of kindness that his father did for people. And it was not just family.

His cousin Rev. Bridge mentioned the fact, that one thing his uncle used to say, that one day all his children will be together, even if it was over his dead body.

The funeral was bigger than just a funeral. It became a great big going home party. As his cousin continued, he mentions that everyone from all walks of life came to celebrate this great man.

Just like anyone else's life, you live through the good times and the bad times as well. The main thing mostly everyone spoke about was how he felt about his first wife passing away on him. It broke his heart.

What broke his heart even more was when he had to split his family, his children up. All of Mr. Bridge kids started crying over that statement.

 Mostly all of them did not truly know how he felt about that. And them. Kind words was also said about the current wife Mrs. Bridge, Jamie.

They acknowledged the fact that Jamie supplied the love and support that Mr. Bridge really needed to keep on keeping on.

 It was a very heartfelt and touching service. When Aunt Debra spoke. That was when for once and for all, a lot of questions were about to be answered.

Their aunt told everyone that Willie knew one day he was going to receive backlash from his kids. On why, he had to split the kids up. He was not sure if he had made the right decision on that. He always called her and spoke about it.

She would tell her brother that everything is going to be all right. He knew the move was made to help the upbringing of his children. Every single one of his children began to cry, major leakage. During the last viewing of the body, Ty viewed his father's body for the very last time.

Ty could not help but to breakdown. It was extremely hard for him. It was like he fainted. The first person he saw that helped him up. Was his brother Jerome. It was like an out of body experience. Ms. Jamie was totally amazed on how Ty-Rome and Jerome look alike. Before anybody could say anything,

Ralph's wife answered by saying all the brothers looked alike. Then she looked at Ralph and said, "Right Ralph!" she said it with a smile on her face. Ralph responded with "Yes," "but only two were born on the same day" Ms. Jamie said that Mr. Bridge always talked about that. But she never saw the two them at the same time.

Jerome, Ralph, and Ty took a little walk away from the crowd of people. Who stood in front of the church where the funeral service took place?

Basically, they stood across the street. They all agreed that one day they all would get together.

With their wives and children and have quality time to get to know each other again. Ralph walked away from the conversation when his wife called him to do something. Ty and Jerome had a nice heartfelt conversation. Both missed each other. They did not even have to say any words.

Ralph came back to the conversation, he said how happy he was when they were born. And how happy they father and mother were also. Jerome explained to his brothers that he will not be attending the burial service that was on the next day. He was not happy about it by far.

But he had to get back overseas. Upper brass orders. They shook hands. Hugged one another. They took a picture together. Ralph's wife took out a camera and took the photo of them.

After that Jerome walked to his government assigned vehicle. Ty and Ralph remained there talking. They watched and waved at their brother as he drove away.

Ralph told Ty that Jerome said as soon as he gets his time in. He was going to retired from the military. The next day, they got into a bunch of limousines. The limousines were there to take them to the burial site. Ty got called Jerome quite a few times. Ty did not mind that at all. He understood it.

Jerome lived out there. He did not. Plus, Ty knew the real reason. He knew if Jerome were to come to New York city, people would think he was him. Ty's sisters and grandparents rode with Ty in the limousine to the burial location in the cemetery.

After the minister said words. And the pallbearer and a couple of the cemetery staff lower the casket into the ground. As everyone began to leave, everyone steps up to the casket and tosses a flower in the casket in the ground. Ty stood over the casket. Looking at it in the ground.

Then he spoke hoping his father could hear him. He told his father that no matter what. He will survive, plus he will never forget him. He will never forget the man, who made him the man he was today. The man who gave him life. The man who never turned his back on him.

He placed a big rose on the top of the casket. Then he said, "I love you pop!" then he turned around and walked away with tears in his eyes. He walked back to the limo; he wiped the tears from his eyes. Ty knew things will never be the same.

They drove away. Ty kept looking back at the grave site. His grandmother grabbed his hand and held it. The family had the after past at his grandparent's house.

While everyone else were eating. Ty called back home. He wanted to check on Dana and Lil Ty. Dana told him; she was happy to hear from him.

And that Lil Ty was fine. Ty let her know that he was leaving late on that night. He told her; he was ready to come home. After he ate. He already made plans. He books his flight back home. He asks his brother to drop him off at the airport.

While he was eating, he held good conversations with various family members. Before, he got into his brother's car. He shook his grandfather's hand. He kissed his grandmother on the cheek.

He promised his grandparents as soon as Lil Ty gets bigger, he would bring him down south, so they could see them. His grandfather told him that he is going to hold him, to his word. His grandmother told him, that they house will always be open to him.

He greatly appreciated that. He talked and received a great deal of love. Even though it started off under sad circumstances. When he left, he felt the love in the air. Ralph also told Ty he should visit more. Get to know his family more. Ty replied by saying he will do that.

When they got to the airport. Ralph made sure Ty got the bags checked in. Ralph waited with his brother until it was time for Ty to board his flight. Before he got on the plane, he called Dana to tell her, he was about to leave. He wanted to give her the arrival time of the plane, he was about to board.

As soon as Dana got off the phone with Ty. She got prepared to pick up Ty later. She got Lil Ty ready. She went to her mother's house. She stayed by there until it was time to pick Ty up from the airport. While Lil Ty and Dana sat in her mother's living room. Ms. Medina noticed that Dana was glowing.

Also, she noticed Dana was gaining weight. Especially around the stomach, breast, and hips. Dana completely avoided all questions.

Her mother asked about that. She was not trying to hear that. But she did ask her mother does she has any food. Did she cook.

Before Ms. Medina could response. Dana was already on the phone ordering pizza. She made sure she ordered enough pizza for everyone who was there at her mothers. Ms. Medina looked at her. She asked her, what was the pizza for.

"Wait, why are we having a pizza party?" "What was the
occasion?" Dana smiled at her mother and politely left the
kitchen. She sat back down on the living room couch. Lil Ty
came and sat on her lap.

She joined her youngest sister and brother who were
already sitting in the living room watching T.V., while Ms.
Medina remained in the kitchen.

Stirring at Dana from a far. The time was going on, she kept
on asking Dana was there something she wanted to tell her.
Dana honestly did not know what her mother was talking
about. Even though she did not know what her mother was
talking about.
She just kept on changing the subject. The delivery guy with
the pizza. He knocked on the door. Dana rush to open the
door. She paid the pizza guy and gave him a little tip. Then
she closes the door back. Dana placed the box of pizza on
Ms. Medina's kitchen table. She asked her mother did she
want a slice of pizza.

 While she already began eating a piece of pizza. Ms. Medina
grabbed a slice. Dana gave everyone a slice of pizza, while
she snacked on her second slice. She did not notice Lil Ty
was looking up at her the whole time.

Finally, she looked down. She broke off a piece of her third slice and gave him half. Ms. Medina could not hold it in anymore. She wanted to know why was she hungry? Was this her first meal of the day. Dana told her mother that she just ate a little while ago.

Ms. Medina was amazed. Because the way Dana was eating this pizza pie. You would have thought she did not eat all day long. Ms. Medina stopped with all the questions about that. She was concerned about Ty. She asks Dana how he was making out with everything? Dana said to the best of her knowledge, he was doing fine.

Both had a concern look on their faces. As they continued to eat their slice of pizza. Dana's little brother and sister kept on coming back for more, more and more. To the point that Ms. Medina, their mother said that there were greedy.

Lil Ty noticed everyone's slice of pizza was bigger than he had, he turned to his mom and looked at her like she had a problem. She noticed his look on his face. So, she broke another piece of pizza from a slice she had in her hand.

He pretends not to see her. He went to his grandmother and pointed at the pizza box. Ms. Medina had a trick for Lil Ty. She pointed at his mother. All he could do was to go back to his mother. To get the piece that was offer to him in the first place.

After Dana gave Lil Ty juice. He was ready to go to sleep. He laid on his grandmother's couch. Before you knew it, Lil Ty was knock out like a light. As everyone got ready for bed, at Ms. Medina's place. Including, Ms. Medina. Dana even started dozing off. She was fighting off her sleep, by watching T.V. Before she drifted away.

The phone rang. She picked up the phone. On the other end of the phone was Ty. He told Dana he just got off the plane. He is in New York at the airport. He will be waiting at the same spot she dropped him off at.

Dana gathered her things, her purse and car keys. She woke up her mother to let her know she was leaving to get Ty from the airport.

While Ty waited for Dana, he went to the newsstand. He picked up chips and a magazine to read. Dana got in the car. It was traffic, but not that much. Normal amount of traffic considering driving to the airport.

Before Ty could get into the magazine. Dana was there outside in the car waiting for him. He saw her when she pulled up from the window. Ty was impressed how punctual Dana was. Dana asked Ty did he want to drive. Ty said, "No."

Dana suggested that they stop off and get chicken and fries, from her favorite chicken joint.

He agreed, he did not see any problems with that. Dana told Ty she wanted to tell him something. He had a what now look on his face.

Still, he asked her what? She said that she would tell him at the end of the week. Then she asked him about his ordeal. She wanted to know about the funeral and everything. Things like how it felt to see all his siblings again.

Ty began with how he loved his family had for him. How such a great man his father was? He did not know many of the things his father had done.

He told her, he saw his grandparents, brothers, and sisters. He was shocked about how many pictures his grandfather had of him. Many pictures of different phases of his lifetime. He told Dana that all he heard and seen really touched a soft spot in his heart.

Dana just listened and drove. She was feeling everything he was saying. Dana stopped the car in front of the chicken restaurant. They walked into the restaurant holding hands. Dana felt a little nauseous, somewhat dizzy. She held on to Ty's hand a little more firmly.

He looked at her to see if she was all right. She said, she was fine. She insisted on that she was fine.

Ty ordered a bucket of chicken to go. For the ride home, Ty decided to drive. Both Ty and Dana were tired. Plus, they agreed on picking Lil Ty up in the morning.

When they got home. They ate a couple of pieces of chicken. Then they got prepared for bed. Dana sat on the couch. Ty gave her a kiss. Then he went to bed. Dana stood up to watch the 11 o'clock news on television. Then she got a glass of water.

She felt the need to eat more. That is when she realized she needed to see a doctor. She needed to check that out. Dana was happy that Ty was back.

She missed Lil Ty, even though she was getting him the next morning. She knew her son was all right. He was at her mother's place. She went to the bedroom.

When she laid in the bed. She looked to her side, there was Ty knocked out for the night. She laid there looking at him, until she too, fell asleep.

Chapter 7

After a couple of days went by. Everything became normal again. Ty was back to work. Lil Ty was growing from a baby to a little boy. Every morning Tanya would drop off Markie. On her way to work. Dana would watch him for a few hours.

Then she would take him to school. Markie was in the first grade then. Lil Ty wanted to do what Markie did. Every morning while they took Markie to school. Lil Ty would grab his spend the night little book bag. Place it on his back.

Sit in his stroller, like he was going to school also. In his little book bag, he had a couple of his toys in it. And one of the little kiddie books that his mother read to him before he went to sleep at night. When they got to the school playground. Lil Ty wanted to follow Markie inside the school.

Dana explained to him, that sooner than later. He too will be going to school. Like clockwork, Dana would drop off Markie and pick him up from school.

Lil Ty could not wait until he saw his old friend, old friend. First, when they arrived back home with Markie and Lil Ty. She made Markie do his homework. Dana gave Lil Ty a coloring book.

So, he could color pictures. That was Lil Ty's homework. That kept him busy. While Markie did his homework. Plus, that was the time when she could start dinner. Like every day, Tanya was over by Dana's around 6 o'clock to pick up Markie.

Whenever she was running late, she would ask her to feed Markie dinner for her. Most of the time, she would come upstairs and talk with Dana for a little while before her and Markie went home.

As they spoke face to face, Tanya noticed Dana's glow as well. Tanya recommended that she check that out. She finished by saying, "Hey, you never know!" Dana told her she had already schedule a doctor's appointment.

Dana's appointment date was set up on the day and time that her mother was off. So, Ms. Medina could watch Lil Ty while she handles her business. The appointment went fine.

The doctor took many tests, just to see what was going on. He told her she was simply fine. Plus, she was expecting.

The expression, the look on her face was an indescribable look that matched her feeling about it at the time. Being absent minded and shocked about what was going on and what had taken place.

She had the nerve to ask the physician, what was she expecting? He chuckled and told her; she is having a baby. While smiling, he told her congratulations. You are pregnant.

That right there, that news right there caught Dana completely off guard. Dana stood there for moment in shock. She was not mad at all. She just had mixed feelings. She knew her and Ty did not plan for this to happen.

They wanted another child. But not that soon. She felt good about at least knowing what was going on. Knowing is half of dealing with it.

When she picked Lil Ty back up from her mother's. She will be able to tell her mother about it. When she got to her mother's a whole lot of other things were going on. So, she decided, she will tell her at another time.

Anyways, she had to go to the school to pick up Markie.
When Tanya came to pick up Markie, Dana told her about it.
She laid the new news on her best friend. Tanya told Dana;
she had already known. She told her, you could just look at
her and tell.

Before Tanya could go on, Dana went to look at herself in
the bathroom mirror. She came out of the bathroom. And
agreed with Tanya. "Girl, I do look pregnant." Then they
both laughed. Dana told Tanya that this time around she
wanted a little girl.

But she will be happy with any sex that the baby came.
Tanya asked her how she was going to break the news to Ty.
Dana kept it real with Tanya. She told her she did not know
yet. That was the question of the day? She was thinking
about telling Ty over dinner that night. She really did not
want to take long time hiding that from Ty. She did not like
to keep secrets when came down to Ty.

Also, this could be something to bring back life in him. It
really did not take a rocket scientist to see the passing of his
father left a void in his life. Dana knew his father meant a lot
to him. This would be a good thing. Tanya told her, before
she left. That whatever she decides to do.

She will have her back regardless. Then Tanya and Markie left for the night. Lil Ty said bye to them. As he stood at the door with his mother. After that, Dana and Lil Ty waited for Ty to come home.

Ty arrived at home at the same time as usual. He was greeted upon arrival from Dana and Lil Ty. He gave Lil Ty a five. He gave Dana a nice kiss on the lips. He thought about putting some tongue in the kiss. But when he looked down, he saw Lil Ty stirring in their faces.

He asked Dana how was she feeling on that day? She told him besides having a bigger appetite, she was feeling simply fine. She asked him was he hungry? And was he ready to eat. Lil Ty told his mother that he was hungry, and he was ready to eat.

Ty looked at Lil Ty and smiled. Then he told Dana he and Lil Ty was ready to eat. While she was making the finishing touches on dinner. Ty went to the bathroom to fresh in up. As they ate dinner, Dana was giving Ty so many hints on her current, status.

She even mentions that one day their immediate family will be getting bigger. She asked him, how did he feel about that? He responded with the day it happens, that is when they deal with that.

Then he looked at her and ask her why she was asking these types of questions. Dana finally broke it down. She let Ty know that they were expecting.

His response, "Expecting what?" She laughed. "Think!" "Silly," "Think!" He sat there and thought about it for a moment. Then he caught on to what she was eluding too. That she was telling him that she is with child.

Ty was shocked. Dana told him she acted, felt, and said the same exact thing. In her response at the doctor's office. Ty was happy with what he was hearing. But he had to be honest, he was not thinking, he was going to hear that. He asked her how many months was she? She told him she was 2 months.

They both finished their dinner. He wanted to know did Dana tell Ms. Medina the good news. She told him; she did not do that yet.

She told him she wanted him to be the first to know. Even though, she knew that was a lie. But a little white lie will not hurt anyone.

Well, that is what they say. Believing that is another thing. They knew that was not true. Ty knew how close Dana and she was, so as soon as she found out, the first person she told was her mother.

She wanted to tell her. She remembered she was going to tell her mother earlier that day. But she got sidetracked. So, she did not. Then he asked about Tanya, she let him know, she had to tell somebody. And Tanya is that somebody.

They laughed like they usually did when they said something slick to one another. They sat on the couch in the living room. Lil Ty sat in his little chair. Lil Ty saw everyone was smiling and happy.

So, he started smiling as well. Even though he did not know why he was smiling for. They sat on the couch cuddled up watching a great movie on the television screen. Ty saw Lil Ty was falling asleep on his little chair.

Ty told Lil Ty to go to bed. Lil Ty did not know how to react to that. He decided to climb up on the sofa love seat. And he laid there. That is where he felt back asleep. Before Ty could respond to that move. Dana went into the bedroom. She got a blanket for Lil Ty. She places it on him.

She went and sat back on the couch with Ty. She got back all cuddled up with Ty. Ty was trying his best not to fall asleep. It was hard especially when Dana picks out the movie to watch. She liked romantic movies, movies with story lines. Ty liked action packed movies. A comedy, they both enjoy watching that. With hard days at work. It really was difficult to stay awoke.

During this romantic movie. Dozing off was all, but too often. During this movie. Sleep was the hunter and Ty were the prey. It was all a matter of time.
Even Dana noticed it. She suggested that Ty go to bed. Ty told her, that he was okay. He could stay awake and watch this movie with her.

After a couple of commercials, he threw in the towel. He gave up. He kissed Dana. Then he bowed out the race graciously. He told her; he was going to bed.

That is where he will be. Dana told him; she knew where he was going. And she will be in there in a little while. She wanted to finish this movie she was watching. He went to the bedroom and went to sleep.

After a short period of time, he woke up to use the bathroom. He noticed Dana was laying on the couch knocked out. He went back to the bedroom and got her a blanket. He left the T.V. on. He turned off the lights.

Then he went back to sleep. A while after that, Dana woke up to use the restroom. She came back in the living room. She turned off the television.

She scoops up Lil Ty, she carried him to his little bed. That was beside her bed. She placed him in his bed. Tucked him in. Then she got into her bed and went to sleep, beside Ty. She went to sleep with a smile on her face. She was pleased on how everything went on that day.

After a normal like weekend, for Ty and Dana. Besides the big news of the weekend. Back to business Monday morning. Ty was back on the job. Whenever he got a chance, he would call home to check on Dana.

Dana liked the fact, that Ty was calling home to check on her. It showed that he, cared about what was going on. To her, he got mad points from her, for that. Even Lil Ty became more helpful as Dana's belly began to grow larger. He was helpful, like he knew what was going on.

Mainly being himself, helping when it was convenient to him. Dana looked out the window, daydreaming into the space. Her moment of getting away.

She was not the type to complaint about life and its circumstances. She looked at life as you must be grateful of what you have. Because it is always going to be people worst off than yourself. Her belief was to be happy with her blessings.

She continued to stare in a daze. Thinking about the future. As she rubs her belly. She waked up out of her daydream. By Lil Ty tapping her leg.

She turned around to look. To see what happened. She asked him what he wanted? He told her he was hungry. She got up and went to the kitchen to get Lil Ty something to eat.

Lil Ty followed his mommy into the kitchen. She began to make him lunch. Lil Ty taps her on her leg.

She asks him what? He pointed to the cookie jar on top of the refrigerator. She looked at to what he was pointing. She looks back at him. He smiles. She told him, "Not now!" he was somewhat confused or maybe that is not what he wanted to hear. He had a puzzled look on his face.

But he was fully aware on what was going on. She made him a sandwich. He finished his sandwich. Just like a good boy. His reward was a cookie. That he yearned. He received a cup of milk to wash it all down. Lil Ty left the kitchen happy and full.

A little happy camper that was what he was. He went back into the living room. To play some more. Being full took its course.

Before you knew it, Lil Ty was laying there, sleeping on the floor, in the middle of the living room. Dana went to the living room.

She noticed Lil Ty was laying there asleep, looking extremely uncomfortable. She placed him on the couch. She sat next to him. While he had his little body stretched out. She watched a little bit of T.V.

As she got into a comfortable position on the couch. While she watches the television occasionally, she would rub her belly. Ty went to lunch with his co-worker, longtime friend, Omar.

 He told Omar the good news. Omar congratulated him on having a soon to be new addition to his family. Ty said thanks to his longtime friend.

But Ty's biggest concern was would he be able to take care of his family. The way he wanted to raise his family.
He wanted his family to live, not struggle. Omar agreed. He understood, he knew what it was all about. They continued to eat their lunch.

They knew before you knew it lunchtime would be over. And it would be back to work time. Lunch breaks always goes by so fast. It felt like the shortest hour in the whole workday.

Ty was a type of man, that he would do any and everything to keep his family afloat. On Saturdays, after Ty gets his haircut. He would meet up with Omar at the shop. They would get their haircuts and hang out there for a while. Sometimes they would stay around until closing.

Since one of their friends was one of the barbers at the barbershop. They would wait until he got off work. Afterwards, they spend time together.

The three of them would go and check out another one of their longtime friends. One of their friends who lived in the neighborhood. The neighborhood hangout spot was their friend Sparky's house.

They knew if anything was going on. It was going on over there at Sparky's place. Either in Sparky's backyard or basement. It all depended on the weather. When the weather got bad. They spent time together in his basement.

In Sparky's basement he had a pool table. Chairs and tables for card games. Workout equipment. They were not the only ones.

It was a whole crew of them who met up over there. There were so many activities for the men to do there. From boys to men, they still went to Sparky's. Some of them grew up and had families.

Others still had their hands, eyes, and feet towards the streets. The majority grew up. Making grown man moves. Others was still living the street life. Getting into fights, getting locked up. Things of that nature.
But overall, that was just a small part of the crew. When it came down to anything, the crew was all for one, and one for all. Everyone went to Sparky's house to have a good time.

Plus, Sparky did not like all that wild and crazy stuff. He felt like crazy and wild bought too much attention to the crew. From way back, they always spent time together. Sparky was the leader. Even though he hated titles. Or the label as being the leader.

Still all of them looked upon him as one. Sparky was the oldest one out of the crew. He was the one, who they could come to for just about anything.

When they had a beef or a problem. No matter what the problem was. Sparky knew how to get things dealt with. Ty told Sparky about his new edition to his family. Sparky brought a bottle of liquor.

So, all the crew could celebrate Ty's new addition. They all were straight up happy for him. That was cool. They were going to buy a bottle and drink together anyway. But this night they tossed it up and toasted to Ty. They all called it Man-time.

Where they chilled, drank, smoke and do whatever they choose to do. Nobody could tell them anything for at least a couple of hours. This week's bottle was in celebration of Ty's big news. Next week they will be celebrating something else.

Some Saturdays either they will watch the boxing match or the Knicks on a big screen T.V. Even Sparky's wife liked the fact, that she knew where her man was. Sometimes, she offered to make some food for his fun night. If the occasion was big enough.

Each man would bring a prepared dish from home, that they wife, baby mother, girlfriend made. Only on major occasions, like the super bowl, the world series, NBA finals.

On normal days they would just order a big bucket of chicken. And call it a night. By a certain time, everyone's woman called Sparky's house to find their men. By a certain time, some of them would be outside Sparky's house waiting for the men to come out.

Sparky's wife would yell down the stairs, sending messages that each one of their women gave. After a while she sent Sparky's son to relay the messages. As usual after a while of that, Sparky would get aggravated with all of it. When that happened, he tells everyone to leave. He told all the crew that he will see them next weekend.

While everyone else was leaving. He asked Ty to stay behind. All of them had good jobs. They all had women and children. Times was not getting easier. Times was getting harder.

If anything, wages was the signs of the time. Ty had an extremely good job. Sparky knew that the salaries that all of them were making was just not enough to really keep an average household.

They all had quote on quote, good jobs. Most of their jobs were good jobs. Their money was a little above average compared to other people's salary.

But times were changing. The economy was going up. And the wages stayed the same. Most of their children's mothers were on welfare. On government aid.

He seriously felt like the only way to make ends meet, was to hustle on the side. He asked Ty what he was going to do with the extra mouth to feed? Ty told him, he has not thought that hard about that, yet.

Ty told Sparky; he will let him know after he thinks about it. Sparky's said, "Well, all right let me know what you're going to do?" He let Ty know he had his back. Ty told him; he knew it.

He was greatly appreciative. He thanked him for the love. And for all of that. Sparky told Ty to tell Dana that he and his wife said, "hi." Again, he told Ty congratulations. Ty left and went home. Ty came through the door of his place.

Dana was laying on the couch with her bunny slippers on. With her bath robe. Ty asked her was she ok? She told him, "Yes, I'm just a little cold" Ty asked her, what was her thoughts on getting a bigger place. She said that would be nice.

She offered to get herself, a part-time job. Just to help with some of the bills. Ty didn't disagree with her. He just told her; they will talk about that on a later date.

 Mainly, after she has the baby. She said," ok!" Ty saw the look in her eyes. His new game plan was to get a bigger place. He thought about what Sparky told him last Saturday.

The whole crew had money invested into the street game. All, including Ty. All of them knew and understood that it took more than a paycheck to survive nowadays.

 All Monday at work, Ty was thinking about ways to make more money. He even thought about getting a second job. Once a month when they met up at Sparky's house. He would distribute money from their investments to each in every one of them, the investors.

To some it was extra side- money, others they really needed the bread. Ty, he really needed the money. When he went looking for a second job. It was not that hard to do. To Ty's surprise.

The time he looked was around the holiday time of the year. He went to this interview for a delivery company. The pay was not great. But it was okay for a second job. Dana was happy and proud over the move that was being made.

The only thing that Dana did not like, she felt like he was not getting enough sleep. That was a concern of hers. On the bright side. Ty was able to borrow some money from Sparky. So, they were able to move into a bigger place.

They got a bigger place at the right time. They moved around Thanksgiving. Perfect for the approaching holiday season. Ty's second job was not that good. One thing good about it was he was getting good tips. Dana was thrilled that she could have her family over by her for Thanksgiving.

Dana told her mother that she was pregnant. Ms. Medina, as usual was a few steps ahead of her daughter. When Dana told her. She just looked at her. And told her she already knew.

She was just waiting for her to tell her. The family plans for the holiday season went like this. Thanksgiving dinner was at Ms. Medina's place. Christmas was at Dana's. New year's party, after church was at Mary's.

At her mother's place on Thanksgiving, she invited everyone to come by her for Christmas. Dana wanted to plan a great big Christmas gathering. Big holiday dinner, etc.

Especially, for Lil Ty. She wanted to have an incredibly special Christmas for Lil Ty. She knew this would be the last Christmas he will be spending as the only child.

Plus, being the baby of the family. Dana was so into planning her Christmas event. The weekend after Thanksgiving she already had her Christmas tree up. She allowed Markie and Lil Ty to help her out with the decorations. Her assignment for Lil Ty and Markie was to make cheerios trimming for the tree.

Shortly after she realized that the boys were eating more cheerios than making the Christmas trimming. She saw what was going on. She just made them a bowl of cereal. Their job was over before it got started. She was fine with that. And so were the boys.

Afterwards, they went back playing as usual. Still, they were able to help in different ways. Like holding this and holding that. Small situations, which was about it. When she finally finished. She turned on the lights on the Christmas tree.

Lil Ty and Markie stood there in amazement. They stare at the lights for a little while. The candy canes did not work either. Every time she left the living room, Markie and Lil Ty would sneak a candy cane off the tree.

When she came back into the living room, she noticed a candy cane was missing. The way it went down was, Markie would be playing with his toy cars. Lil Ty would grab a candy cane off the tree. Then he would bring it to Markie, so Markie can open it for him.

Part of the deal that was made was for opening it up. He had to get a piece of the candy cane, as well. Lil Ty had no choice but to agree to these terms.

Markie would open the candy wrapper, break the candy cane in half, and give the other part to Lil Ty. Dana went around the apartment looking for the boys.

When she caught up to them. She said to them, "Hey, where did them candy canes go?" "Whose, been stealing my candy canes?" she said next. She looked at Markie and Lil Ty. "I'm waiting for an answer?!"

When Lil Ty turned around to face his mother. He had a mouth full of candy cane in it. She asked him where did he get it from? Lil Ty had so much candy in his mouth he could barely open it.

Since he could not response that way. He shook his shoulder, like he did not know what was going on. Markie stood there confused and everything else. She did not go hard on Markie. Because the missing candy canes were at the bottom of the Christmas tree.

In Lil Ty's reach. Markie played it off like he did not know where it came from. He probably thought she gave it to Lil Ty for them. So, he just opened it and gave his god brother half of it.

Dana was not angry or anything. She just knew for a future reference; she should have the candy canes out of reach.

Every night, Lil Ty waits for his mommy to cut on the Christmas tree lights. He stops whatever he was doing at the time. Just to stare at the lights. He loved the fact, that occasionally, the lights would change colors.
When that happens, he gets excited.

Lil Ty also noticed that his mother stomach was getting extremely big. Sometimes during the day, she would stop what she was doing. She would sit down and rub her stomach. Everything with Christmas was going as planned. She even received her first Christmas gift to put under the Christmas tree.

The gift was from Ty's job for her. She placed the small attractively packaged gift box under the tree. She went to the kitchen. Normally, Lil Ty would follow her. She notices that he was not behind her.

He stayed in the living room playing with his toys. So, she thought. He played with his teddy bear that he takes everywhere with him on the living room floor. After Dana got dinner started. She went to the living room to sit down for a bit.

She began to watch the television. She looked around to see what the Lil boy was up to. Because Lil Ty was too quiet to her liking.

She wanted to know what was he up to now? She began to scan the whole living room with her eyes. She saw his right leg, there was a piece of wrapping paper under it.

Another piece of wrapping paper was in his hands. He was playing with the wrapping piece of paper like it was one of his toys.

Dana got up from that couch to go to him. She called him by his whole name. He pretended like he did not hear her. She called him again, still no response. When she got close enough, she tapped him on his little shoulder.

"Where's the gift that was under the Christmas tree?" She said it in an angerly voice. He gave her this look, like he could not understand what she was saying. That look did not help him, not one bit.

He must have forgotten that he had some wrapping paper under his leg. She did not care about the wrapping paper. She really wanted to know where the gift was.

She went searching for the actual gift. She went into Lil Ty's bedroom. And there it was, the gift. It was found on his favorite teddy bear.

She noticed the scarf wrapped around the teddy bear's neck. When she first looked in his toy chest. She saw the teddy bear, but she thought nothing of it.

Then she realized that this teddy bear did not have a scarf.
The icing on the cake was the scarf still had the shopping
tags still on it. She could not do anything but laugh about the
situation.

she knew it was truly funny. She knew what she had to do
about that. Lil Ty thinks every gift under the Christmas tree,
he is supposed to open. She tried to explain to him, that all
the gifts under the Christmas tree was not just his.

She saw he really did not understand anything about this
process. Things like gifts is supposed to be open on
Christmas day. Later, when she told Ty the story. Both found
humor in it.

Still, they came out of it with, they cannot place any gifts
under the Christmas tree until the night before.

So, Lil Ty could not get to the Christmas gifts. The best way
to avoid Lil Ty and his mischief.

Chapter 8

The year ended on a good and sour note. It was good
enough to end the year with a smile on everyone's face. As
planned, Lil Ty had the Christmas of his life. Dana was so
happy; she was able to give everyone in her family a gift.

Especially happy when Ty got her the set of earrings she
wanted. Ty was happy with the fact that he was able to
make his lady and little man happy. This stood for the good
side of the coin.

The sour part, the second job he obtained for the holidays.
When he went to pick up his check. It was a note attached
to it. A Lay-off paper was stapled to his check.

The company's manager told Ty he did a really good job.
And he should apply next year. To work next year with them
for the holidays.

 He ended his conversation with Ty with saying they would
love to have him back next year. If he needed a reference, or
a good word, he should feel free to get into contact with
them. Ty thanked them for thinking about him. That was
cool, that was peace.

He knew from the start that the job was just a seasonal job. He just wished and was trying to make that into another opportunity.

All the while it did serve its purpose. He could not be mad about anything. Still, he could not help but feel some type of a way about it. His next move was going to find something like the work he just finished. And plus, great second job hours.

He knew, he needed the extra money. Knowing he about to have another child. Who will be born in this world very soon? Still with hope, tomorrow will bring a new day with new opportunities. Dana was getting closer and closer to her due date.

When they say the first seems like the longest. Ty felt like Dana was pregnant with Lil Ty forever. Dana being pregnant this time around, it was moving so fast, it was almost an unbelievable rate.

One good thing about the beginning of the new year, was tax season was right around the corner. When he received, his w-2 forms from his jobs, that he worked last year.

The return was good. Thank God because they really needed the money. It was extremely helpful at that point of time. Just like all money, the money came and went.

Luckily, for Ty, he was able to invest some money into the streets to stretch his money a little bit further. Investing into the streets, He took Sparky's advice about that.

Instead of just being an investor. He figured out; he wanted a piece of the action. To participant in the actual drug game hand to hand operations. He gave Dana a part of the money to save for a rainy day.

Certain things Ty liked to keep away from Dana. That was one of them. He always wanted to keep her from any hurt, harm or danger. He did not want any drama or struggle that he could avoid. The thing about life was that life keeps on moving forward.

Today becomes yesterday and tomorrow becomes today. That is how time is. As they say, as the world goes around. When it comes to this thing called life, tomorrow is always dictated with today's thoughts.

For the most part. It sounds good, too bad life is never that easy, nor that simple. The thought of life, having its own twist to it. That is the way it goes. Nobody for certain knows what tomorrow may bring.

Dana went from a small belly into a big belly with the course of time. Just like the first time, Ty was at work when he got the call to come to the hospital. He rushed to the hospital. He went straight to the delivery room.

Everyone was there, like before. Ms. Medina, Tanya and stepmother came. Ty's father Mr. William B. Bridge was not. He passed away. At this point of time, Ty really did not have any positive male figures in his life.

He knew his father was not going to be able to see this childbirth in the flesh. He knew, he was there in spirit. He knew his dad would be proud. Proud of the birth of his new child. Not so proud of his movements.

One thing for sure, Ty was not running away from his responsibilities.' Being responsible, that is what real men do. Dana gave birth to a healthy baby boy. They decided to name the baby after Ty's father. The baby's name was William B. Medina.

They still did not use Ty's last name. Just in case if they needed public aid. The way the government was set up. It was just easier to get necessary help if needed, that way. Food stamp did help in a time of need.

It did help when necessary. The way the jobs were paying, nobody was above the poverty level. The cost of living went up. The pay checks did not. As soon as the hospital allowed it, they bought Lil Ty to visit his new little brother.

Lil Ty was ecstatic to be a big brother. He told his father, that he would like to keep him. Ty looked at Lil Ty, as did Dana, then looked at one another and they began to laugh. Lil Ty stood there with a blank look on his face.

 Because he did not get the joke. You could say it was way over his head. He did not know any better, when he said what he said. As Ty took them home, On his way home from work.

When they got home, he took a long look at what he had. Not monetary, but the physical. His family is his great responsibility.

The next level of life. Being the head of the household. One thing he knew for sure, he never wanted to be in any predicaments of letting them down.

That was his goal, his mission. At the end of the day, Ty did not want to hustle on the side. He preferred to work for his pay. The fact of the matter was he would do any and everything it took to support his family.

No matter what the cost and the price was that he will have to pay back in the long run. Lil Ty got use to his little brother. He loved the fact, that it was someone there that was smaller than him.

That he could look out for. Summertime was a great time for Dana and the kids. Dana made sure Lil Ty enjoyed himself that summer. She took them everywhere she could think of.

They went to museums, local parks, amusement parks, places for kids to have fun. They even went to Coney Island. Dana loved the fact, that whenever she gave Lil Ty something. He offered some to his little brother.

Even though, he could not have it. He was not big enough. But it was the thought that counted. You could not help but to love Lil Ty. On how he felt about his little brother. Everybody he met, he told them about his little brother, the baby.

All W.B. could do at this point of time was eat, cry and smile. Remember, that is what babies do. They went to the beach and pool too. Lil Ty really enjoyed the summer. When they were not traveling having fun.

She made sure Lil Ty knew things like counting to ten. How to spell his name. A little bit of the alphabet. Things of that nature. She wanted him to be prepared for when he starts kindergarten.

Which was in the coming fall. She knew September was right around the corner. Dana was going to make sure Lil Ty was ready. Dana was that type of mother.

She liked to be ahead of the game. She got started in June with the basics. When Ty, Lil Ty and Markie go to the barbershop on Saturdays, Lil Ty would ask could W.B. go too.

That part was cute because W.B. wanted to go too. The funny thing about it was W.B. did not even have hair like that in the first place. He was just growing his hair. Some weekends he took all the boys including the baby to the barbershop.

All the men in the barber shop could relate to it. A baby at the barbershop, all the guys was so into it. W.B. was sitting there relaxing in his stroller. Somebody even offered to make the baby a bottle.

Ty declined the offer. But before he declines, he asked his friend, did he even know how to make a bottle?

He said no, but he will call his wife to bring a fresh bottle of milk to the shop. They all laughed about that one. Ty said, for all of that, he could just call the baby's mother to bring by a bottle. He was grateful that his friend thought about him and his baby.

Another one of his friends got on the friend who suggested getting the baby a bottle of milk. He told him; he knew that was a dumb idea in the first place.

All the friends could do was to agree. He felt maybe he should think it over a little before he said what popped inside of his head.

After Lil Ty got his haircut. The barber gave him a lollypop. He asked him could he get another one for his little brother. The barber gave him two. Lil Ty did not know that Ty was looking right at him.

On the way home, Ty asked Lil Ty for the extra lollipop that he had. Lil Ty was shocked that his father had caught on to that. As they continued their trip home. Lil Ty had this look on his face. The face of being in trouble.

Markie told Lil Ty a story about how he tried the same thing and Ty caught him. He let his little God brother know that he felt his pain. But at the same time, he found it very funny.

Ty pretended like he was not listening in their little conversation, as he walked pushing the baby stroller. He turned around and gave Markie the lollypop. Markie asks him for what. He told Markie for being a good guy.

When he reached the corner of the block. As he waited for the traffic signal to turn to the walk symbol, so he could continue walking. He turned around again and gave Lil Ty a lollypop as well.

The traffic light changed, so they continue to walk towards home. Dana was sitting on the stoops talking to Tanya. They were talking waiting for the crew to arrive from the barbershop.

When the boys reached the block. They saw their mothers sitting there, so they ran to them. Ty remained walking at a normal pace, pushing the baby stroller down the block. They reached their mother. They check out their haircut.

They liked it. Tanya told Markie she will be back in a little while. When she gets off work. Tanya came on her lunch break from work. She had to go back. After Ty said a couple of jokes. Dana got scared and check the baby. Ty stood there and laughed.

Because he told her he got the baby a haircut. She told him, he may be a little stupid, but she knew he was not crazy.

She also told him that she knew he was not playing with a full deck. Then her and Tanya went back to their conversation.

While Ty took the boys upstairs to get some juice. The baby stayed downstairs with Dana and Tanya. As they continued their conversation until Tanya had to leave to go back to work.

Then Dana called Ty downstairs to get the baby stroller, while she walked upstairs with the baby in her arms.

Chapter 9

Work was work. On the streets, now that was another story all together. Ty rented some space from Sparky. He sold his weed out of it. He bought the weed in weight. He bought it from Sparky. He brought along his long-time friend, his partner in crime, Omar. Omar invested as well.

Also, he worked with him this caper. Their own little daily operations. They always had a couple of dollars in it, here and there. But this time they had both feet in it.

Now, they wanted to play more of a hands-on game. They wanted to be where the real money was. A bigger piece of the pie. Within a few weeks, they had a couple of workers, working for them. It was not moving fast. But not that slow either.

Until Ty hired this kid name Spotty. When Spotty started running the operations for them. That is when they started making real money. Spotty explained to Ty if they packed their weed bags to full ability.

Having the weed bags looking like little, small pillowcases. He told him their product would move quickly. Because everyone was out there looking and wanting a good deal.

They agreed to try it out. Long and behold, the customers started coming like water.
Products were moving.

They only rented the spot for a couple of hours. 4pm to 8pm, was their hours of business. When it was Ty's turn to put his work in the spot.

No matter, how much work it was. They always sold out within a couple of hours. When Ty met up with Spotty every night. Spotty had a bag full of money and sold-out results. He gave it to Ty at their met-up spot, the Chinese restaurant.

While they sat in the restaurant eating some food, Ty went to the pay phone to call Sparky. He needed to re-up on some work. More product, the daily re-up. Even Sparky was amazed, at the same time impressed, how fast they were moving the product. The money kept on pouring in.

The summer was great, not like any other. Ty got to treat his woman like a queen. And his children like royalty. The way he always wanted to. Things he only dreamed about doing he now was doing.

Finally, he felt like he was making some type of progress. Ty was smart about everything. For example, when you bought drugs from the spot, you did not see any of his workers faces. They had a loose brick on a step, on a group of steps.

You move the brick, then you tell them what you wanted, as you slide the money through the hole in the step. Then you received your product. Then you must place the brick back the way you saw it. No visual contact.

So, you do not know whose selling it. The people in the neighborhood did not have a clue, who was selling. They knew where it was. But had no idea, who was involved. Out of sight, out of mind. That was the motto. That was the key to success.

Also, Ty understood time frames, when to sell, and when not to sell. At first, the 4 hours was a good enough time for them to do their thing. When their operation was in effect. Ty and O made sure they were across town, far away from the spot.

Most of the time they were still at work on their regular jobs. Definitely, no one thought they had any parts of it at all. Omar liked that. Plus, the type of money that was being made.

The workers understood, the more money the spot made, the more money they would make. Operations as whole was doing well. Towards the end of the summer. Dana got Lil Ty registered in school.

Now it was all about getting him ready for his first day of school. Preparing him to be in school all day. Dana, Lil Ty and W.B. went back to school shopping. Ty left a genuinely nice amount of money for school shopping for Lil Ty.

Dana felt like it was a little too much. But she used enough for shopping. Lil Ty was excited to get new clothes, a book bag, new sneakers. On top of that, he was ready to go to school.

After seeing Markie going to school. All Lil Ty wanted to do was to do what Markie was doing. He saw how much fun Markie was having. All he wanted was a part in that.

With all the preparation, Lil Ty was ready for his first day of school. He was ready all the way to the actual first day of school. That is when he got scared.

Dana pushed W.B. in his stroller as they walked with Lil Ty and Markie to school. Markie went to his new class line. Lil Ty looked nervous.

Dana walked Lil Ty to his new class line. Dana kissed him on his cheek. She told him, that he was her big boy now. She talked him into giving this a try. The first bell rung.

The principal came outside. The principal placed the bullhorn to his mouth. Then he spoke into it. He welcomes all the new kids to the school. Also, he welcomes back the kids that already went there.
All children lined up with their classes.

They began to walk inside the school grade by grade, class by class. Dana remained there with all the other parents. All of them had tears in their eyes. Waving bye to their children.

Dana was no different. Dana stood at the gate with tears in her eyes. She was worried, proud, and excited all at the same time. She stood there for a moment. Then she looked inside the baby's stroller to see what W.B. was doing.

He was sitting there chewing on his sleeve. Dana thought W.B. would have been asleep. But he was not. So, when she looked at him. He looked back at her and smile and laughed. She wiped her teary eyes. Then she smiled back at her baby.

On her way back home, she stopped at the park. She sat on the park benches for a little while. After that she stopped at the neighborhood deli. She picks up a couple of things. Things like cheese, eggs, and whole wheat bread. She went home from there.

When she got back upstairs, she made herself some breakfast. She made a bottle for W.B. She turned on the little television that was in the kitchen. And she sat down and ate her breakfast watching T.V.

While she was feeding him his bottle, he would sip and smile, sip, and smile, that was his thing to do.
She told him, that he would be next. The next one to go to school. He looked at her and smile and sip his bottle. He kept that up until his little belly got filled. Then he was ready for his nap. He fell asleep with the bottle in his hands.

Before she allowed him to go to sleep. She made sure he burped. Shortly after, he needed a diaper change. As she watched the daily soap opera on television. W.B. was laying on her knocked out.

The sleepiness became contagious. She had dozed off too. She took a shorts nap. After the afternoon nap, she got herself and W.B. ready to go pick the boys up from school. As the bells of the school rung. Dana was standing there in the yard with the rest of the parents. W.B. in his stroller in front of his mother.

The classes began to come out. Markie's class was one of the first classes to come out. Markie went over to Dana. Dana asks Markie to navigate her through the crowd to where Lil Ty's class would be. Lil Ty's class stood on the other side of the school yard. He stood there online with the other children.

The line he was on got shorter and shorter. He could not help but notice, everyone else's family got most of his classmates. Soon, he found himself feeling like he was not wanted. He felt some type of way about that. It was just him; a boy and a girl were left on the line.

He begins to stare at the ground. He paces a little bit. He kicks a little pebble that was on the ground. Not wanting to be at that place at that time.

When he looked up in the crowd. He saw his mommy pushing his brother in his stroller. And they were coming his way. Markie was leading them through the crowd of people. Dana and Lil Ty caught eye contact with one another.

Before Dana could reach the line, Lil Ty was on. Lil Ty ran up to her. He gave her a great big hug. Gave Markie a hand slap. He waved to his little brother in the stroller. Dana asks Lil Ty to take her back to the line he was on. She told him she wanted to see his teacher. She wanted to meet her.

When the teacher turned around trying to figure out where Ty-Rome went. Dana saw the teacher's face when the teacher turned around. She noticed it was the same teacher that Markie had a couple of years ago.

Markie had her in kindergarten. Seeing who the teacher was, gave Dana a sign of relief. She has dealt with this teacher before. She knew that teacher was an exceptionally good teacher. Lil Ty will learn a lot in her class. That was great news for Dana.

Lil Ty was happy with satisfaction with the teacher. He told his mommy; the teacher was fun. When they got home, Lil Ty told his mother everything that happened in school that day. He wanted to tell her all about what happened on his first day of school.

Before Dana told the boys to change into their play clothes. She got the camera from the draw.

She wanted to take a picture of this moment. Lil Ty was happy. He had so much fun, he could not wait to go back to school the next day.

What he experienced the first day of school, got him ready for the next day. School started on a Thursday. The first two days went by extremely fast. Saturday was here. Saturday mornings, TY would take Markie and Lil Ty to the barbershop with him. Just like always.

When they came into the shop Ty would walk around and give everyone a five (a handshake). The boys copied his moves. They both looked up to Ty. They wanted to be like Ty. Before Lil Ty used to be scared to get a haircut. Now he could not wait to get one. Ty did not know if Lil Ty wanted the haircut or he wanted the lollipop, that he received after.

If Lil Ty got it done. Ty did not care what it took. He liked getting a haircut so much. He felt like if his father gets a haircut, he should get one too. Ty would tell Dana that he was going to the barbershop.

Before he could put on his jacket. Lil Ty already had his jacket on, standing at the door. Waiting on Ty. Dana was extremely impressed that Lil Ty liked getting a haircut.

Until Ty busted the bubble with the reason Lil Ty really wanted to go the barbershop. He told her that every time Lil Ty got a haircut, they would give him a Lolli pop. Dana was like, "oh okay!" "So, that's the reason why he was into the haircut thing." She said to Ty, while looking at Lil Ty.

Then she said, "I should have known." Lil Ty pretended like he was not listening to their conversation about him. Ty told Dana he will be back. Dana told Lil Ty to put his jacket back where it was at before.

Before he could even frown up. Dana already planned for him to help her make some cookies. His interest completely changed gears. He was more concern about making the cookies than what or where his father was going. He totally forgot about the barbershop. Lil Ty sat back down on the carpet.

He began to watch the television again. He remained quiet until it was time to help mommy with making some cookies. Where he sat at, W.B. was in his walker. He stepped towards his big brother.

Then he sat in his walker and watched the T.V. with his brother. Lil Ty whispered into W.B. ears, that their mommy was about to make them some cookies. W.B. did not know or understood what Lil Ty was talking about.

W.B. did not know what the good news was. But he read Lil Ty's facial expression. So, he was happy and excited, that Lil Ty was happy and excited.

Dana looked at W.B. and asked him, why was he so happy? Because he cannot eat cookies yet. W.B. looked at his mother confused and then he laughed and smile at her. Like he always did.

Saturday began a little slow, mainly preparing and baking the cookies. With the baking process. It was plain to see Lil Ty was not too much interested in that part. Until it was time for him to eat the cookies. That is when he was so concerned and involved. After he ate two cookies, Dana told him that was enough at that point of time.

She did not want him to spoil his appetite for later. She knew in a couple of hours, he needed to eat his dinner. She did promise him, that if he ate his dinner, he could have another cookie.

He did not completely agree with her. But he knew that was the only way to get another cookie. He knew, he had to behave as well.

That meant, do not bother mommy about cookies. Lil Ty went into his room. He got some toys, so him and W.B. can play with. Dana and Tanya were on the phone.

Tanya was telling Dana how big Markie got. She told Dana; he was almost her height. Dana was like, who you are telling! Tanya wanted to thank, Dana and Ty for taking out time with Markie. Dana told her friend; you're welcome any time.

Also, she mentions to her was the last time she checked; the boy was her god son. Tanya agreed. Tanya was on her lunch break. Tanya was on her way to get a burger and fries from a fast-food restaurant. She asked Dana did she want anything from where she was going.

At first, Dana was going to say no. then she thought about it. Then she said yes, to the offer. Tanya told her; she will pick it up for her. And she will be there in a little while. After that, they got off the phone.

Right after that, Lil Ty asked her what was they having for dinner? She looked at Lil Ty and ask was he listening to her phone conversation.

He looked at her, he did not know how to answer that question. "Nope!" flew out of his mouth. She knew he was not telling her the truth. She was slightly angry at him. She told him to get a book to read.

He went into his room to get a book from his little bookshelf. He sat on the couch with W.B., she sat between them. She took the book and began reading it to them both. Just about every other page in the book. Lil Ty had a question about the book.

She told him the next time he will be reading this same story to her and his little brother. That got him to pay attention more. He sat back, listened, and looked at the words as she read them aloud. W.B. rested his head on her arm. Just looking observing and of course having no response. Reading to her kids.

Well, that was Dana just being Dana. Sitting there with a good book in her hands. Reading to the loves of her life, her babies, her children. When the story was over, Lil Ty wanted more of the story.

Unfortunately, that is how the book ended. He told his mother; the book was a good book. Then he asked her when he will be able to read any of the book. She lets him know; it will be sooner than later.

She told him to place the book back on the bookshelf. He did that, then he came out of the room with another book. "No more Today," "And put that book back too!" she said to Lil Ty. She turned on the T.V., She placed W. B. on her lap. She turned to the television show, she and her kids enjoyed watching together.

While they were watching the T.V. show. She heard the door buzzer. She went to her intercom and ask who it was. It was Tanya at the front door. So, she buzzed her in the building. When Tanya knocked on the apartment door.

Dana opened the door for her. Tanya brought some bags from the fast-food restaurant. Markie followed behind her with a bag full of soft drinks.

Tanya suggested since they were there, they might as well eat there. She asked Dana would that be all right to do so. Dana looked at her and said, "Girl, which will not be a problem!"

They both laughed at one another, because they knew, they both was being silly with each other. Dana and Tanya sat in the kitchen. Dana brought out some paper plates.

While they set up the food for the boys. The boys were in Lil Ty's room playing. Like they always did. Lil Ty wanted Markie to read him a book. Markie wanted to show Lil Ty this new game he got.

But it was too advance for Lil Ty to grasp the concept of it. Lil Ty watched Markie play the game. W.B. hung out with Dana and Tanya in the kitchen. He wanted to be where the food was.

Until he got bored of being there. Then he stood up and his walker and traveled where the boys were playing. He wanted to see some action.

W.B. day consisted of him, his walker and being all over the place in the apartment. A couple of times a month, Dana would take the boys to church, on a Sunday.

She always kept herself neat. She always dresses genuinely nice and neat. Her children looked healthy, neat, and well taken care of. Lil Ty always had a fresh haircut.

As she grew older, she gained a closer walk with her spiritual side. Her religion, her faith. Her mother, Ms. Medina always encouraged her to do so. Dana's mom was remarkably close in her faith with God.

She installed into her children to seek God for guidance. Her belief was, if they put God first in their lives, everything else will fall into place.

With God in your life anything and everything is possible. God will always make a way for you; all you must do is believe and pray.

For Dana and her siblings, faith was second nature. They always had these words of encouragement. As Dana grew in womanhood, and a mom. She realized that God keeps everything in order. When they attend a church service. Lil Ty would sit and keep an eye on his little brother.

Whenever Dana had to do something during the service. It was not like they really were alone. In the row ahead of them is where their grandmother sat.

Occasionally, he will check on W.B. to see what he was doing. Both the boys liked church. Especially, when the church was singing. They enjoyed clapping their hands. Dana felt complete when she attended. She knew, she needed it too.

Like her mother always said, it was important for a woman to have faith in God. The understanding that no matter what, God is and will always be in control.

The first thing a person must do is to believe. When it comes to God, belief goes a long way. Everyone needs some type of faith, higher power in his/her lifetime.

Sunday would end with a nice home cooked family dinner. When dinner was ready, Ty and Lil Ty would sit at the table. W.B. would sit in the highchair. They ate dinner together like how normal families do.

Nice conversations, if it was Ty talking about his work week, Lil Ty was talking about school and schoolwork. Or Dana would talk about her week. Also, how W.B. was doing. Family time was the best times in one's life. Memorable events become precious and priceless moments that stand the test of time.

They loved that time. Just like anyone else. After dinner they would have dessert and sit back in the living room and watch a movie. Lil Ty would try to hang, but with a full belly. His task was nearly impossible.

After a while of fighting, he could fight no more. He had to give up and go to sleep. When it came down to Dana or Ty, it was a toss-up, who was going to wave the white flag first. Depending on who you ask. True be told, whoever was more tired. That is who went to sleep first.

Everyone needs to get some rest. The next day was the beginning of the week. Lil Ty met so many new friends at school. For a few days it was hard. He enjoyed going to school. Him going to school was no problem. The problem was when it was time for him to do his homework.

He wanted to play around with it. He would keep on playing and playing until he notices his mother was not playing him. When Dana hand the belt in her hand. He regained focus on the task at hand, quick.

With him seeing the belt, concentration was no problem. Daily routine, Dana and the belt vs. Lil Ty and homework. W.B. had a front row seat to this show every day. Some days everything went smooth and fine. Other's well that was a different story.

Those days Lil Ty had to suffer the wrath of Dana, because he chose not to do what he supposed to be doing. Just like clockwork, W.B. began to grow teeth. As time went, W.B. began to walk. Talking came into play also. Now, W.B. and Dana walked Lil Ty and Markie to school.

Lil Ty always gave his little brother a five. Before he walked into the schoolyard to get in his class line.

W.B. liked how his big brother treated him. Kindergarten was a big challenge for many kids. Mainly, getting use to the school routine. First grade was a little easier, not for the homework part.

For the routine part about it. Ty knew what he must do. W.B. would cry when it was time to leave Lil Ty, at the school yard. W.B. was just being a little brother. Dana knew Ty was making a lot of cash.

She barely questioned it. She knew he was a hustler. A jack of all traits. She always told him to be safe out there. Plus, make sure he comes back home in one piece. That is all she cared about.

At the end of the day, she wanted him to be safe. She wanted to make sure he got back home, their home. She really did not care about all the other stuff. And nobody could tell her any different.

Most people knew this about her. That is how Dana was and is going to be when it came down to Ty. To all of them, why bother telling her anything about this man. Because she was not going to listen anyway.

It was all about her and her man. That is all she knows.
Whoever did not like this for some reason. Then that was on
them. And really Dana did not care how anyone else felt
when it came down to her and Ty.
It was about how they felt about one another.

Chapter 10

As usual Ty came home from work. By a certain time of the day, Lil Ty and W.B. stopped what they were doing to listen out for the door. They watched and waited for the keys to jiggle from outside.

When they heard that sound. They watched for the doorknob to move. The opening of the door behind that. The boys made sure they cleared a path from the door. They stood far but near the door.

When Ty got into the house, Lil Ty and W.B. followed him into the living room, where Dana was at, sitting down watching the evening news on the television. Then both boys gave their dad a five.

After greeting their dad, Lil Ty went back to doing his homework. And W.B. climbed up onto the couch next to his mother. Ty went up to Dana and gave her a kiss. He went for her cheek; she turned and planted a big one dead smack on the lips. He smiled, she smiled.

After Lil Ty completed his math homework. He went up to his father to tell him how his day went. Ty sat down and listen to what Lil Ty was saying. Lil Ty told him how the whole day went at school.

From the beginning to the end. Ty looked on impressed. At least you knew what you did in school for the day. Ty felt like that is what counted. Lil Ty was ready and willing to carry on. He was about to, until Dana told him to go back to his little desk, which set out in the Livingroom.

She wanted him to finish all his homework. Or he knew it would be major problems. Again, he sat down at the desk and got focused. Ty asked Dana, how did her day go. She told him it went well. She wanted to know how his day went also. He went on to say it went fine as usual. He asked her about dinner.

He wanted to know what she cooked on that day. He picked up W.B., and he asks her about him. How was he coming along? He looked at the kitchen. Dana looked at the kitchen. They both looked at the kids. The kids looked at the kitchen.

Then they looked, and the kids looked again. That is when they realized that the kids were copying off them. That is when they laughed amongst one another. They also copied off that, they laughed as well. Everything was all funny like a joke.

Until it got serious when Dana told Lil Ty to get back to his homework. Lil Ty thought he could get some sympathy from Ty. His father agreed with his mother. So, he definitely didn't have a leg to stand on. The best thing for him to do, was to get back to his homework. And he knew it too.

Especially, after Ty told him to listen to his mother. That was enough to put him in line. An ordinary day, an ordinary life, just like anyone else's. Life is so similar but different. Yet everyone goes through almost all the same predicaments.

The weekend came, Dana went out with her sisters, Tanya, and a whole bunch of friends. Ladies' night was still in full swing. The only thing that could consider a change of plans, was if someone's children or child got sick or something like that.

 Even if one of them had to work. No one, nothing could derail their train off their tracks. They still went out; even though certain individuals could not make it. Because of different reasons. Some had to work at the last minute.

 Or they stayed home for various reasons. The event still went on. Nobody was stopping the show. Their lady's night out was amazing.

For their friends and family members who missed their functions. They always took pictures of the good times, that they were having.

Most of the time, they had to pick the children up at Ms. Medina's. Which they had to pick them up after they went to church. Most of them would pick their kids up after morning service. Ms. Medina kept Lil Ty and W.B. with her.

They had to go with their grandmother back for the afternoon service. The boys had no choice in this matter. If Dana had set plans for the boys. Then Ty and Dana would pick the boys from after the morning church service. Who if they were out and about?

Whatever the case was, they would eat dinner as a family. They would have a family day. As W.B. got bigger and bigger. Dana could not wait until W.B. got big enough, so she could return to work.

Dana really did not care about being a stay at home, mom. Staying home was not her thing. She always preferred to work.

At this point of time, she knew if she went back to work. It would be extremely costly. It would cost more money than they had to spend.

At WB's age, to babysit him, would cost almost a paycheck to do so. The game plan that Dana and Ty agreed on was, when W.B. gets big enough to go to kindergarten then she will return to the workforce.

Every once and a while, Ty would come home from work and complaint about being the only one in the household that was bringing money to the table. Going on about being the only source of income.

Which totally ticked Dana off. Then other times, he told Dana she did not have to work. That she did not have to worry about money because he had this. To Dana, it was a bunch of mixed signals thrown her way. She went with the flow, for the time being.

The agreement was both their children were too small to be thinking about extra moves. They clearly were not ready for no transition, for now. They knew once their kids got a little bigger everything will fall right into place.

Dana did like having a hands-on experience with her children. Dana really wanted to make a job move. She had a bunch of family members who would be great choices to watch and babysit the kids?

Ms. Medina enjoyed spending time with the boys. She always told Dana watching the boys would not be a problem when she was not working. Ms. Medina felt like her grandsons were easy to deal with. She liked the fact that her grandsons listen to her.

Well, to the best to their abilities. Boys will be boys. Ms. Medina knew and understood that. W.B. always liked when he went by grandma's house. He loved the fact, that his grandma would put a little sugar in the oatmeal.

Plus, on certain days she would cut some fruit and put it in the oatmeal. Those days W.B. did not even want to go home. Lil Ty enjoyed going to grandmas also.

Lil Ty felt like his grandma was more fun and fair-minded, when it came down to what he wanted to do. Lil Ty would talk about that with his mother. Dana always asks her mother about that.

She wanted to know why she did that. She wanted to know the fact on why she was so lenient when it came down to her grandkids oppose to her own kids.

That puzzled Dana. Dana could not understand that for the life of her. Such a simple question got a simple answer. Ms. Medina told her that it was easy to explain.

First, your kids, your problems. See with Dana and her siblings that was her kids. Dana's the parent now. Now she was the grandparent. Grandparenting was a much easier job. That was the parent's job to discipline the children.

The grandparents' job was to have fun with the kids. She let Dana know she was just about done raising her own kids. It is up to them to raise their children.

Ms. Medina's motto was, I will watch your kids for a little while, but after that, you must get your children. All Dana could do was laugh.

They both knew she was dead serious though about the matter. Dana started doing odd jobs from home. Things like babysitting, doing hair, etc.

Dana wanted to earn her own money. She felt better as a person making/ having her own money. Dana was always an independent individual. That is just who she was. Even Ty knew that about Dana. Which he admired.

In fact, he respected her about that quality. The way he helped her out was by buying her any needed supplies. He was completely supportive of what she wanted to do. Dana had quite of few talents. She was always good at doing people's hair.

Hairstyling came natural for her. So, it was not a problem for her to get someone hair to do. She had a couple of hair clients.

Ty business operations was going according to plan. Instead of just hustling part-time, for him and his partners. They decided to rent the spot, a couple of days of the week.

Not a few hours of a day anymore. Now they wanted a whole day. It was simple and sweet, no one ever expected them out all the people in that neighborhood to be selling drugs out of that corner building. He remained far away as possible from the daily operations.

So far, it made it virtually impossible to pin that on him. Even if they tried to. Ty besides being about his family, his money, and his life in general. Ty was also a very smart, intelligent man in his own right.

Most people did not know that about him. Because he came off less intelligent. That was his way of throwing people off. He made it his business to make sure people did not see the intelligent side of him too often. With people not knowing how smart he was.

Which made it extremely easy to outsmart a fox, the average person. Which made him have the advantage over many more than a few.

After years of working for the moving company. The owner of the company passed away. The old man, Mr. Ville left his company to his children.

They tried to run it for a couple of years. Even though realistically, they knew nothing of running the company. Plus, they really were not interested in running the business. The very same business, they father put his blood, sweat and tears in. He owned and ran the moving company business for over 30 years. Before he passed.

After serious consideration, they decided what was best for them, which was to sell the company to someone else. With the negotiation they produced. Was the only condition the new owner had to allow all employees who work there, continued to work there? The new owner agreed to the terms.

With the signature on the contract of bill of sales. For all the employees, which was great news. Over the fact, that they still had a job. Unfortunately, different management came along with different ways and actions of conducting business.

The new owner tried to keep most of the old contracts the company had for years. Some of the other companies took their business elsewhere. Instead of giving the employees extra overtime, which was well needed to make a living for themselves.

The new owner decided to cut hours and overtime. He also cut down the workload and work crew. He then cut the workday into shifts. So, yes it was the same company. At the same time, all the workers were being paid less wages. Everyone made less money.

Due to this fact, many was forced to leave. Ty was not happy with the way things were going either. The cost of living just kept on rising. Times were rough. Times were hard.

Especially, trying to raise a family in it. Ty knew hustling was not a good thing to do. But he also knew, you had to do, what you had to do. That was the bottom line of it all. The less money he made at the job. Since the legit money was low.

So, he had no choice, he had to switch to survival tactics. To produce the rest of the money that was necessary. Necessary to keep himself and his family above the water. That is the way life goes. Money do grow on trees. But not in one's hands. You must go out there and make and get that money.

While he hustled and worked. Ty was always looking for a better job. He was constantly looking for a job. Which was exceedingly difficult to do at that point of time?

The struggles he faced was not in the plans at all for Ty. What he was doing was not what he set out to do. But it did pay the bills. Job interviews mostly ended in dead end situations. Everywhere he went, nobody, nowhere were hiring.

That did not stop him. He continues to look for a better job. He did not give up the search, even if he got shut down. In the meantime, his thought process, his thinking cap were leaning more towards hustling for dollars. Sparky told Ty that things was getting hot for him. Sparky caught word on the streets about himself.

People was talking about Sparky on the streets. Someone informed the police officers about Sparky's activities on the street. It all started when a group of guys got arrested on some drug charges.

 The police officers began doing their little investigation on Sparky's operations. They wanted to take down Sparky. Even though no one they interviewed would give any type of information about Sparky.

To the crew knowledge. Yet, someway, somehow, Sparky got arrested on some drug charges. The police officers arrested him when he came out of the local bodega. When he asks why they were arresting him? They told him that he knew why?

They took him to the police station. They wanted to question him further. For all the questions they asked him. They got no answers in return.

All they did was go back and forth with it. Neither side was going to crack. Even after numerous stare downs. Finally, they told Sparky what he is being charged with. They really did not have anything on him, except for a couple of firearms he had in his vehicle.

Even though they arrested him coming out of the store. Not in his car. But while searching him they found his car keys. And they illegally searched his car. That is when they found the illegal firearm.

Because technically they we are supposed to check his car. They did it anyway, even without a warrant. Still, they placed the guns into evidence. That is why it was shocking to Sparky and his defensive team when the judge did not throw out the gun charges.

The prosecution offers him a plea deal. If he wanted to take it to trial. That was on him to decide. The judge remanded him. With no bail. He gave him a court date in a couple of months.

Sparky and his lawyer felt like they could beat the charges, because the police officers overstepped their boundaries. They had no authority to search his vehicle. So, the search was illegal.

To them they had a strong case against the prosecution team. That oversaw the case. For now, Sparky understood, he was on ice for the moment.

While he waited on his court date. He asked Ty to visit him on Riker's Island. He wanted to talk to him. They spoke for a while, not saying much.

Mostly in code words. They knew they were surveillance cameras all over the place. They were fully aware of their surroundings. It was obvious they were more than likely listening to their conversation.

Before Ty left, Sparky was able to say what he needed to say to Ty. Ty got the message. The message was that he placed Ty in charge of the whole operations. He wanted Ty to hold down the fort until he got out of jail. What they thought was going very quick and easy.

But that was not the case, the judge offered him 2 to 4 years in prison. His lawyer recommended that he take the deal. So that is what he did. Sparky knew he would be able to get out less than 16 months. The man called Sparky remained on ice.

With that happening. Ty began to make even more money. Ty now had contact with the main connect. The main supplier, the main source. He was now able to obtain and ship out bigger packages.

He had to supply the whole operation now. Not just his, but the whole movement. Sparky wanted that way. So that is how that went down. Ty knew how to throw Dana off. He just told her that he got another second job.

 Once he said that, she did not question about his whereabouts. Her time was occupied anyway.
Her sons were enough with just keeping up with them. Was more than enough for anybody.

Days came and went. After all the job applications that Ty had filled out. Ty finally got a call back from one. They called him to come down for an interview. The job was a particularly good job, a great opportunity. Much better than the job he had.

Ty was happy and was looking forward to the interview. He had told Dana about it. When she heard the good news. She began to get excited about it. He did not want to get anyone hopes up too high, too soon.

Ty was slightly concerned with the fact; he knew he could not hustle forever. He knew he had to make a next move. With all that was going on. He was just going to ride and enjoy the wave that was supplied for him.

He was going to get it. While it was able to be gotten. Even when they raided different spots, now and then. The police officers captured a few of his workers. But they did not know too much, to begin with.

Most of them were so low level, they did not know who Ty Bucks was. They could not pick him out of a line up. On the streets they knew him as "Bucks'". That allowed him the opportunity to elude the law for years. When Sparky went up for parole. They denied him. He had to serve some more time.

The next time he will be able to go to the parole board would be another 2 years. Ty kept his word with Sparky. Ty always sends Sparky a package and money to him in jail. On the streets, he helped Sparky's wife and kids get through these difficult times.

Ty understood, no matter what he did, he had to stay ahead of the game. And always a few steps ahead of the law. He knew any slip up or mishap could land him in big trouble.

He was not trying to hear that. Plus, he did not want to experience that. Freedom was especially important to him. Ty and Dana lived on the third floor in a three-family duplex, across town.

Far away from where he did business. They lived on the top floor, so they had access to the roof. Some nights Ty would take his fold-up chair to the roof. He would sit and stir at the stars, to clear his mind. The perfect place to be at.

Out of sight, out of mind. He had a little table he kept up there. Whenever he wanted to have a business meeting with his top lieutenants.

They would have the meeting on the roof. He brought a couple more fold up chairs for that occasion. His homeboys, only the trusted individuals were allowed.

Most people did not know about this place. The place that Ty Bucks lived at. Some nights, he will stay up there the whole night, until dawn broke. Just thinking of the next move. That he knew had to be made.

On Valentine's Day, he dropped the kids off to Ms. Medina's place. To Dana's surprise, he invited her up to the roof. At first, she did not want to go. But he persuaded her as usual. When she got up to the roof, she was surprised by a romantic candlelight dinner.

Where they sat at, they were able to eat and look at the stars in the sky. Dana loved it. Even though it was a little cold. Ty noticed that, so he took off his jacket and gave it to her.

Now with the proper wear for the occasion. The concentration was on the fact, that love was in the air. Carefree, from this depressing society. That they lived in. The reality of it all.

After dinner, they embraced the darkness holding one another. The night was perfect. The night cap was self-explanatory. A night of passion followed, until the morning time.

Ty picked up the boys the following morning. He came with a box of chocolates for Ms. Medina. He also gave her a card with some money in it. Ms. Medina thought that was so sweet of him.

It was back to work for Ty after he dropped the boys off to Dana. Dana took Lil Ty to school. Ty just worked the job he had for fun and the cover up.

Besides, he been lost love for the job, he was working on a long time ago. Work was work, he still had to try to at least make an honest living. W.B. was just about ready to go to school. Dana began to get him prepared for that.

Just like she did with Lil Ty. Dana taught him how to count to the number 10. She taught him how to spell his name also. Plus, some of the alphabet. W.B. always sat next to Lil Ty while he did his homework. W.B. wanted to do what his big brother was doing.

Dana's Godson Markie got so big. Big enough where Dana did not have to babysit him like she used to. He could watch himself at home. Lil Ty went to the fifth grade. And W.B. began kindergarten.

As this took effect, Dana was able to work a part-time job. She would work a couple of hours a day. She helped in a clinic. Working with patients' files. And other necessary duties.

She was the secretary's assistant. It did not pay all that great. But it was a start and that is what Dana was looking for. That was what she wanted for the moment? It gave her flexibility. She had enough time to go and pick up her kids from school.

She was able to avoid paying babysitting fees. That was a good thing. Besides, they did not have the extra money for that anyway. Everything else was normal. Dana had time to cook dinner. Time to make sure her kids did their homework.

After their homework was done. And the food was ready, she fed the kids. Gave them their baths. Then got them ready for bed. Afterwards, she sat on the couch, watched T.V., and waited up for Ty. Ty came home a little while later. When he got home, she went into the kitchen to heat his food.

While she did that. Ty went to the bathroom to freshen up. After he took his shower, he placed on his pajamas. Then he went into the kitchen. He sat down and ate his dinner.

Ty and Dana had a light conversation, nothing heavy. Sometimes she would wait and eat with him. Other times, he was on his own. Most of the time, she winds up eating with the kids.

It all depended on how she was feeling for the day. After dealing with her new job, the boys with their homework and everything else. Some days, she would be so tired after all of that. She went to bed and went to sleep.

After everything was done. When that happened Ty did not bother her. He went into the kitchen and heated up his own food. He understood she had a lot on her daily plate. Dana was happy with the fact; she was able to make her own money.

Without taking time away from her kids. It was a solution where everyone benefits for her. W.B. adjusted to school very well. There were no problems there, with that. Dana was amazed, that W.B. liked school. The most unbelievable part of it all was the little boy like doing homework.

She felt relieved she did not have to threaten him to do it. Lil Ty now that was another story. That was a constant work in progress. For Lil Ty it was not his schoolwork.

 The problem was when he got home. Sometimes he did not want to do his homework. Dana barely got any phone calls from the school about her boys and their activities, or any reviews about their schoolwork.

Knowing that, Dana was available to work more. She did not have to worry about the progress of her boys. That was a lot off her mind.

Chapter 11

After numerous neighborhood complaints. The captain of the local precinct decided to address this problem. The lieutenant placed police officers Smith and Nickels on the case.

The police department had to attack the drugs being sold on the streets. The drugs in the neighborhood got out of hand. They knew they had cut down the trafficking of the drugs on their local blocks. The police officers were assigned to see what they could produce.

Officer Smith knew Ty, Omar, and the rest of their friends from way back. He knew them since they were little boys, playing the streets.

Ty and Omar always felt like Officer Smith always had it out for them. Officer Smith felt like them boys were always, up to something. Problem kids always getting into trouble.

Basically, in a nutshell, he really did not care for that group of guys. Everything that went down wrong in the neighborhood, he felt like someway, somehow, the group of boys had some type of affiliation to it. Most of them including Ty would just try to avoid any contact with that police officer.

Nobody had anytime to play," Cops and robbers," with Officer Smith. Everybody in the whole neighborhood knew of him. Nobody in the neighborhood wanted any dealings with him. Most people felt like he was at war with the people in the community.

 The sad part about it was the people were not at war with him. Everybody just wanted to mind their own business. He was like a G.I. joe police officer. He was going hard on everybody for no reason at all.

 Officer Smith had many complaints about the way he policed the neighborhood. The police commissioner liked the choice of officers that the lieutenant chose. He had like the fact, that officer Smith was going in a neighborhood that he knew very well. Perfect candidate for the assignment.

If anybody could gain control over the drug problem, it would be him. Or at least, get some straight answers and facts about who to go after. They needed someone to get to the root of the problem. For them, that somebody was Officer Smith was their guy for the job.

The police department did not have to worry about corruption with officer Smith. As he began to narrow down his search.

He and his partner produced a 5-block radius. That was where the main drug strips were found. Where the heart of the problem was. With a few informants they got.

They knew the exact street where a high volume of drugs was being sold. Still with all of that going on. Ty remained out of sight, out of mind. No matter what officer Smith thought, he could not place Ty at any of it. Let alone a drug house.

Especially, when the crack spot was what they were trying to find. And shut down. The upper brass was more concerned with getting the crack off the streets.

They did not really care that much about the weed spots. On one corner was the crack spot and on the opposite side of that same block was where the weed spot was.

Both was on the same street. Some people in the neighborhood called that block the strip. Everyone knew that. To make their presence know, officer Smith parked his patrol car in the middle of the block. So, they can be visible to everyone.

They wanted a bird's eye view of it all. They sat in their vehicle and watched how everything was unfolding. They did not have a clue about who was in charged. Or anything like that. With there being police presence on the strip, people avoided the strip completely. It did not matter that they were in an unmarked vehicle.

Everyone knew what time it was. They were not fooling anyone. Ty was informed that the police were on the strip. With that knowledge, that he received. Ty's decision was to instruct all clients to go buy weed from another one of his locations.

For the meantime. The other spot was just a couple of blocks away. This how they did that, the workers who would normally work inside the spot. He instructed them to stand on the corner and direct their traffic to the next spot. Since that spot was under surveillances. The way to still conduct business, was to take the business elsewhere.

His workers blended right in the crowd at the corner because it looked like they were just spending time together on the corner. Which drew them, no attention at all. The officers thought nothing of the guys on the corner. They produced nothing on that day. They saw nothing suspicious.

After a while, the police officers felt like they were wasting their time. It was like, they were waiting for something that was not about to go down. Even the crack spot was closed.

The strip was a ghost town. Due to the heat the police provided. Ty drove past the police vehicle officer Smith was in. Officer Smith spotted he at once. Since officer Smith and his partner had nothing better to do. So, they pursued Ty. They began to follow his car.

After following Ty for a block and a half. They put their police sirens on. They ordered Ty to pull over his vehicle. As police officers walked on the side of his car. Ty saw who they were, from looking, into his side mirrors. He knew officer Smith from anywhere.

Officer Smith walk and all. All Ty could say was "Damn!" Ty knew Officer Smith, but he did not know his new partner. In Ty thoughts, his partner must be a newcomer. He looked all nervous and everything.

Plus, Officer Smith always used to roll alone. Nobody in the police force wanted to be seen with him. Let alone be his partner.

The police officer came up on the passenger side of Ty's car. Ty had his window down already. The officer walked up to the window. He asked Ty for his license and registration. Also, his insurance card. What the officer asked Ty to do, he followed the instructions that was given.

Ty informed the officer that he was going into his back pocket to get his wallet. That is where his license and registration was. Then he let them know he was going into his glove compartment to get his insurance card. They allowed him to do so.

He noticed, from the corner of his eye, while he was getting his information together, officer Smith had his gun drawn out on him. He pointed his gun close to Ty's head.

Officer Smith ordered his newcomer partner to go to the police cruiser to do a check on Ty's paperwork. Also, to check and see if he had an outstanding warrant.

While his partner did that. Officer Smith asked Ty how was he doing? He seemed like he wanted to have a conversation, that he really did not want to have. As officer smith talked, Ty remained there silent.

The only thing Ty wanted to know, why was he being pulled over for? When Ty asked him that. He answered him with an attitude. He said, "we ask the questions," "not you!" Officer Smith threatened Ty, by saying if he heard anything about him.

He had no problems taking him down. He also, told him any of his paperwork that his partner is checking was not legit. He is going to arrest him, right now on the spot. Officer Smith promised him that.

Ty got a little tight over that. But he knew the best way to shut him down was to say nothing at all. After the two of them having moments of stare downs. Officer Nickels came back to the car. He handed Ty his information. He informed Smith, that Ty's paperwork came back clear.

Then Nickels preceded to tell Ty he could go. Before officer Smith walked away from Ty's car, he told Ty that he will be watching him. Ty said, "whatever!" "what's new!" When Ty said that officer Smith ordered Ty outside the car.

After words were exchanged, officer Smith threw Ty onto his car. He told his partner to pat him down. He wanted to see if Ty had any weapons on him.

While Nickels checked Ty out. Officer Smith checked inside Ty's car. Officer Smith was trying his best, to find anything inside the car. He even checked his car trunk. Still, they could not find anything on him.

They had no choice but to leave him alone. The officers got back into their police car and drove off. When Ty got back inside his car. As the officers rode off from him. Ty just smiled at them.

Then he drove away as well. Ty headed to the Chinese restaurant, where he met up with his affiliates.
Ty was heated about what just happened. He spoke about officer Smith.

Mostly all of them knew officer Smith was a piece of work. They were not shocked at all about what Ty had just met. They all had run-ins with officer Smith one way or another. Ty informed the crew that he was going to lay low for a couple of days. It was simple to do anyway. Everyone knew their positions. And how to play them.

That was the last thing about which he was worried. The thing he worried about was officer Smith's radar. He knew that was not a good look.

He knew, Officer Smith was going to be on him like white on rice. On that note, Ty rather officer Smith watch him, than his operation.

Ty knew he was not really touching anything. The most he did was drive pass his spots and collected money at the end of the day. Ty kept his daily routine basic. Go to work and then go home.

For the next couple of weeks was kept simple. A couple times he did ran across officer Smith and his partner. They stopped him a couple of times. While they spent their time watching him. The spot continued to be up and running with no police interference.

Before you knew it, business was running as usual. After a couple of weeks following Ty around, they finally got the hint that they were barking down the wrong tree. Harassing the wrong person. They decided to move on. There were more crimes to be solved.

Ty felt the pressure was being lifted off him. He also knew not to sleep on the possibility that they can be still watching him from a far. Ty watched his back on the moves he made.

At least, for the time being. Ty was not into playing rush and roulette. When he was not driving through the neighborhood checking on things. He would just go home.

When he came home inside, he would be greeted by his sons. And a hot cooked meal from Dana. Things that what else could a man ask for. Being embraced by his woman. Ty knew, he did not need to be in the streets. The money will be made on the streets.

Without him, being on the streets. That is what the police officers did not understand about the game. Dana was happy Ty wanted to be home more often. She did not have any problems with that.

When Ty was home, Dana always felt better. To her it was less worrying about him being in them streets. Ty laying low was not a problem at all. Ty had other things on his mind than to play, "Cops and robbers," with the police.

He was not going to consume his time, mind, energy into any of it. The day of his big job interview came. He came prepared. He wore a nice suit, shirt, and tie. Fresh haircut. Nice shoes to top it off.

Dana loved the way he looked in his suit. She kept on staring at him. So much so, Ty asked her was anything wrong. She told him that he looks good.

She dwelled on the fact; she was not used to seeing him being dressed up. She asked for a kiss, he gave her a kiss. Then she asked for another one, he gave her another one. She had the look in her eyes. She wished him good luck on his job interview. Ty quickly got out the door. Because Dana looked like she wanted tear Ty apart.

Ty got to the place where the interviews were being held. When he reached the building that he supposed to report to. He was greeted by a security officer, at the front desk. He asked Ty for what he was there?

 He told the security guard why he was there. The officer instructed him on what floor to go to. The female security guard complemented him on the way he looked and was dressed. He presses the elevator button.

Then he stood waiting for the elevator to come to the floor he was at. The elevator reached, he got in and pressed the button for where he needed to go. When he got off the elevator, he went straight to the receptionist desk.

The receptionist told him to sign his name on the list that was supplied for signing on the receptionist desk. She told him after that, he could have a seat until someone comes and deals with him, shortly. He sits down, he began to look around the office.

He likes what he saw. The office looked great to him. Everything was well placed. Ty sat back and enjoyed the scenery and the wait.

He grabs a magazine from the shelf they had on the wall. A couple of minutes later, a gentleman appeared coming from the back of the office.

He got to the waiting area and then called Ty's name. Ty responded, then he followed the man to the back, like the man asked him to do. He took Ty to another waiting room. He gave him a couple of papers to fill out, while Ty began to fill out the papers, the interviewer told him he will be back shortly.

Ty filled out all the paperwork to the best of his abilities. Then he waited for the man to come back. The interviewer came back, he read what Ty placed on his application. He asked Ty for his ID, he needed to make copies of them.

After he came back with the copies of Ty's IDs. Then he asks Ty to follow him into another room. Then he told Ty to wait for him. He knew it was protocol.

He kept it professional. He knew it takes time to get processed. He understood, he wanted a slow Yes. Rather then, hear a fast No. His father always used that saying. As the interview went on.

They both came out of it, with a good interview. Ty felt like they had a good conversation. The interviewer also complimented Ty's suit. He told Ty that he felt Ty was the type of person, that this company needed. The only thing that was left was a background check.

After that he will place him in the next training class. Which the training class starts in two months. But he told Ty to listen out for him. He might be hearing from him, sooner than later.

The main thing they were waiting for was his back-ground check to come back. Ty left the interview in good spirits. Ty felt like, he was finally making some progress. He really did not have to worry about any references.

He knew a lot of professional people. That would vouch for him. The three he chose, was very professional, successful people. People who want the best for him. His criminal back-ground check was decent. Not too much was going on with that.

Besides some little run-ins with the law. Nothing that serious. Things like fare hiking tickets. Nothing major. If you left it up to officer Smith, you would have thought Ty committed murder.

The way officer Smith be up in his face. Dana wanted to hear all about how his interview went. He told her it went well. Dana asked him did he get the job. He told her, he did not know, yet.

He did mention that phrase It went well as planned. The job he had applied for did not have a drug test. Ty really was not worried if it did.

Yeah, Ty sold weed, but rarely did he smoke weed. He knew for a fact, that he did not have any drugs in his system. That was another thing, which was less to worry the brain about.

He knew landing that job was a waiting process. As he waited, it was back to reality. He had to deal with what he has at this point of time. The job he already had. On his regular job, his supervisor was acting strange, as usual, towards Ty.

But Ty was hip to his game. When it was drama on the job, he did not feed into it. He did not pay it any mind. Because Ty knew, the supervisor acted like that with everyone who worked there.

Ty felt maybe it was his turn to get picked on. So, he found it to be quite humorous. Back to the street side of things, the hustle.
The drug spot began to get hot. Just like any other spot that was making money. One day it was hot, the next day it is not. That is just how the game goes.
Even officer Smith and his partner was on some, now you see me, and now you do not, shit.

The police department finally gave up on their little drug taskforce operations, for the meantime. With the police department backing off. The police harassment in the neighborhood dropped dramatically.

The hood became calm. That was good news for Ty to find out. His thoughts on it were maybe they got bigger fish to fry.

Nevertheless, he felt a sign of relief because they were not following him around the neighborhood. Ty was able to chill and relax for a change.

Just go with the flow of life. His daily motto was you must keep on keeping on. Things were going to be all right. Today was a good day. And he was looking forward to it being an even better tomorrow.

Of course, with God's blessings. Because no one's promised tomorrow. Lil Ty was constantly growing. W.B. was not that far behind either.

Dana was buying clothes, giving trash bags away of clothes just as quick. Ms. Medina offered her a suggestion, maybe she should buy the clothes a little bit bigger.

So, they could at least have room to grow in the clothing. That was a good idea, instead of constantly buying new clothes.

Dana agreed and that is what she did. Sneaker for the boys, well that was another story. You cannot buy sneakers that much bigger than their feet. That could mess their feet up in the long run.

Certain things Dana was able to hold on to. Like some jackets and coats. After Lil Ty grew out of it. That is when W.B. was growing into it. Some money was saved in the process. Dana never had any problems with getting money from Ty.

 Ty was not a cheap man at all. If she wanted it, he would give it to her. If he did not have it at the time. He will have it for her later in the day. Dana was never into spending money recklessly.

Dana was kind of old fashion when it came down to spending money. Dana life was about living and loving the family her, and Ty has created.

Dana and Ty got into arguments just like any other relationship. No relationship is perfect. The key to their relationship was communication. It was beyond just being in a relationship. They always held a great friendship based on honesty and trust.

Mainly respect for one another. They learned the fact, that sometimes things might not go their way, or as planned. Believing, trusting, and understanding that on any given day, either one of them can lead the way.

Dana was not the type of female who feeds into outside gossip.

People's opinions on her and Ty's relationship. That is one thing she did not play around with. She loved her privacy. Ty was a private person also. Maybe that is why they made a perfect match. Where there is a start, there is always an ending, not far away.

When it comes to luck. Luck does not last forever. You avoid things as much as possible. Still judgement day is and always will be right around the corner. The police never really stopped their investigation.

Heavy surveillance was still on that matter. Officer Smith and Officer Nickels began to place the pieces together, one by one, piece by piece.

They learned so much with the help of informants. Piece by piece, brick by brick, the operation that seemed unbreakable, got broken.

For Ty it started out as a normal day. A bit strange to say the least. Ty was not feeling this day at all. Compared to the way he would normally be.

He received a message at work, that the spot was running out of work. They needed more bud to sell. They told him they would be completely sold out by mid-afternoon.

While at work, Ty called his connect. He ordered his shipment right on the spot. He set up the transaction to go down at 6p.m. That gave Ty enough time to go home, change his clothes, stop at the spot get the money.

All this was going on within an hour of him getting off work. He was really rushing to get everything done fast. He forgot his wallet. He left it in his work pants back home. As he continues, he did not have any I.D., license, or his personal money on him.

Luckily, he did not get pulled over by the police. He understood that police officers would take something so simple like that and make it such an extremely complicated ordeal over little things like that. He did hurry back home to get his identifications.

Since he was home for the moment. He decided instead of getting fast-food, he will just make himself a cold cut sandwich. After making his sandwich, he went into the refrigerator to get something to drink.

The pitcher of juice he saw, was WB's juice, the one he liked. So, he went deeper into the fridge, to see what else was there to drink.

Since, he noticed that WB's juice container was low. He made a mental note to himself, to pick some more juice on his way back home later.
He poured a cup of iced tea for himself. He ate his sandwich and drink his drink. He went back to finish the running around he had to do.

Before he left the apartment, he made sure whatever he turned on, he turned off. He got back into his car. Then he traveled to the meet up spot. The meet up spot, him and his connect agreed on.

He went to handle his business. He buys his new shipment of drugs. When Ty went to drop off the new work. He would park his car blocks away from the spot. He would then continue through the back way.

He would go through a couple of backyards. Hop over a couple of fences, just to get to the spot. He made sure it was nearly impossible to follow him. Nobody could tell where he was going and what he was doing.

When he got there. He told them to sell out what they still had leftover. Before they began to sell the new shipment of work. When they ran out. Close the spot for an hour. So, they can bag up the baggies.

Then he went to his other spot to pick up some money. He called his connect again. This time he took Omar with him, to hold him down. When Ty got to the deli to meet up with his connect. Omar was there next to Ty with his hand on his trigger of his gun. Just as a precaution.

When you are making drug transactions, anything can happen. Ty pulled out the cash and bought the product. The connect got the cash. And Ty got the drugs. Then everyone went on their own way. On, the way back to the hood.

Ty and Omar stopped at a designated location to bag up the baggies for this spot. They were getting it ready to sale on the street.

Ty told Omar that he will be back. Omar told Ty on his way back, he needed to pick up more baggies. Ty said cool, he took the other pound of weed off the scale. Where he was preparing for weight sales.

He broke that couple of pounds into different packages by the weight. The wholesale part of the game. Ty asked Omar did he want to come along.

Omar declined, he said he wanted to stay there and bag up the rest of his baggies. Ty took a couple of half pounds, a couple of quarter pounds. And a whole pound to sale.

Since he was out there, he figures, he might as well drop off the pre-ordered weight packages. Ty placed the pre-ordered packages in the trunk of his car. He then drove off, to handle his business.

While he was delivering his packages, he decided to stop at the shop that sold the baggies he needed. Most of his packages were sold by then. Most of the money was collected also. He had one more quarter pound to drop off.

Then he will be finished with that part of his operations. When he backed up his car out of the store parking lot onto the street.

As he drove off, he noticed a police cruiser was following him. He did not know, if or why would they be following him for. To make sure he knew what was going on, he decided to make a right turn.

The police car also made a right turn. Ty made a left turn at the next corner, shortly after. While all of this was going on. He made sure he was obeying the law in this process. Rules like signaling, completely stopping at stop signs.

Still the police car was following him. The next right turn, he made. The police car made it right behind him. At this point of time, the police sirens came on. They ordered Ty to stop his vehicle. They told him to pull over to the curve.

Ty knew, he thought about it. But he knew if he tried to make a run for it. That would have made it worst for himself. Ty was much smarter than that.

So, his strategy was to see if he could talk his way out of it. He looked at it like this, hey, you never know! He did not want to over think it either. Ty pulled his car to the curve. The police officers got out of their patrol car. They came up to the window of his car.

One of the police officers asked him for his paperwork and driver's license. The other officer asked him, did he have any weapons on him. He told the officer," No!" Then the officer followed his partner back to the police car. They went to check Ty's paperwork.

After running his license and registration. They came back to Ty's car. They let him know that everything was fine. They did not allow him to move. They would not leave him alone. They told him; it was one more thing they had to do.

Ty looked at the officer, who was saying all of this. Ty was trying to listen to what they were talking about amongst one another.

Ty wondered what will be next. Surely, he was confused about the whole ordeal. Then they told him to step out of his vehicle.

Ty did not understand, why would they ask him to step out of his car. He could not help, but to ask them why? They ordered him to step out his vehicle again. So, he did. He did not want to create a further notion, that he was not following their demand.

Even if they did not have reasonable cause to search him. After they search him. They searched his vehicle. After searching inside the vehicle, they found nothing.

Then they asked him to open his car trunk. That is when they found what they were looking for. They found a quarter pound of weed. As they search him, they found two thousand dollars in cash in his pockets.

They at once arrested Ty. Another police vehicle came rolling up. While they were escorting Ty to the police car. The police officer who was the driver the other police car was officer Smith. Officer Smith made sure he caught eye contact with Ty.

Officer Smith got out of his police car. He walked up to Ty and arresting officers. He asked what they had on him. Why was they arresting him for? They told officer Smith what they were charging him with. Officer Smith looked at Ty again.

He told Ty, "Sooner or later," "I was going to get you.!" He was looking for a reaction from Ty. Too bad, he did not get one.

Nevertheless, officer Smith was happy with the situation. He salutes his fellow officers. He told them; it was a good job.

Also, he told, he was glad they took some street trash off the streets. He walked up to Ty and said something slick, "Now, you can be with your friends, your buddies." Officer Smith, after he made that statement to Ty, he still waited for Ty to respond. Ty did not.

He even had the nerve to call Ty a jail bird. Ty was not in a laughing matter. But officer Smith was. He laughed and told the arresting officers to get Ty out of his face. After all the nonsense. Ty reached the police station extremely late.

By the time they took his fingerprints, it was too late for him to be transported downtown to central bookings. He had to wait until the next morning. The only thing he was able to do was to call home.

Which he really did not want to do. But he had to let Dana know, what was going on. When Dana picked up the phone, she asked him where he was. When he told her where, he was? She pauses for a moment.

Then she asked him what did he do? He could not tell her what exactly he was being charged with. he knew one thing for sure, he would not be able to see the judge that night. He did tell her, hopefully he will be able to see a judge the next day.

Before Dana got off the phone with Ty, she told him that she loves him. And for him to be safe. That was Dana's reaction with Ty on the phone. Her fascial reaction was completely different. The way she felt about it was also different.

If looks could tell it all. You would be able to see she was completely pissed off with him. She did not understand why Ty was in jail. She was not happy about it at all. She did not even know exactly where he was.

That is how she explained it to Tanya on the phone. She had to call someone to blow off some steam. Tanya understood, but she did not want to get all stress out about Ty's personal problems. She comforted Dana by saying, it might not be all that serious.

Dana did not really care; she knew she was mad as hell with Ty. Tanya decided to talk less and listen more in their conversation. She realized that was the best move to make, at this point of time.

After a while of blowing off steam, Dana finally was able, to calm down, for the moment. She thanked Tanya for being a listening ear that she really needed.

Tanya said, "Girl I know if it was me," "you'll be there for me!" then began to talk about other things. That was good because Dana needed to get away from that problem for the time being. With the help of Tanya, it was a good temporary relief.

It worked at first, still on the down-low, Dana was still tight. Dana was upset with what had happened, and at Ty.

In the back of her head, she could not wait until he comes home. Because she just wanted to give him a piece of her mind. Deep down inside, she was missing him already.

Mainly worried about not knowing the whereabouts of her man. Tanya told Dana to get some sleep. And to let her know what the outcome will be tomorrow.

Dana agreed, maybe she was just tripping over the whole situation. Before they got off the phone, she told Tanya that she is just going to put it in God's hands. Tanya followed that with an, Amen.

Then the two long-time friends got off the phone. Lil Ty asked his mommy where was his daddy? W.B. stood next to Lil Ty also concerned. She had to think quick, she told the boys that daddy had to work late. She looked at the clock. She ordered them back to bed. It was bedtime.

She tried to get some sleep too. She could not sleep a wink that night. She remained on the couch watching the T.V. for the rest of the night. Omar noticed that he did not hear from Ty. Plus, Ty did not show back up with the baggies.

He knew something had to be up. Because that was not how Ty moved as an individual. Omar backtracked everything Ty said he was going to do.

Everyone said they received their package, except for one. He told him; Ty did not drop off the quarter pound as promised. Omar went to take care the rest of the business.

Even though it was late, Omar called Ty's house, to see what happened to his partner. She told Omar what had happened. The fact, that Ty got arrested but she did not know why? Omar was surprised to hear that. But was not surprised.

He knew why he could had gotten arrested for. He told Dana that everything is going to be all right. Omar knew even though Ty was behind bars for the moment, the business still had to move on. That is the way Ty wanted it, and the whole crew knew that.

Omar told Dana; Ty was going to be okay. Plus, they probably do not have any sufficient, substantial evidence on him to charge him with something big. With that, being said, she felt a little better about the whole ordeal.

After Omar got off the phone with Dana. Omar was trying to piece what happened to Ty all together. He knew Ty could not have caught with such a big package, cause mostly everything he left with got sold. Omar thought Ty is probably going to need to get bailed out.

 So, he began to get some bail money together. Just in case if Ty needed it. Omar knew in the morning; everyone would have a much better understanding on what has happened tonight.

Then they would know what to do, and how to respond, to what has taken place. For this night at hand, there was nothing anybody could do, but wait until the morning, including Ty.

While Ty sat there in a little jail cell at the police precinct around the way. All he was able to do was to think about was what had happened up until this point. "Damn!" rolled out of his mouth. He knew this did not happen to him at this point of time. He only had one person to blame, and that was himself.

While he was speaking to Dana earlier in the evening, he asked her to call his job, to tell them he was not coming in tomorrow. He made sure he told her that during is one phone call that was given to him.

Dana called his job; she did what was ask of her to do. She made an excuse, she told them that he was sick. And he will probably be out for a couple of days. The secretary told her to tell him to feel better. Ty sat on the hard bench, he laid down, trying to get some type of rest.

Which was almost impossible to do? He really did not know what to expect going through the system. One thing for sure he knew he did not want to be there. The cell he was in was dirty and harsh. Of course, the water fountain was not working. Rust all over it. The toilet did not flush, that too was rusty.

Basically, a long steel bench was bolted to the floor. That was where he sat and laid at. Ty was dealing with his circumstance like anyone else who was in this predicament. He knew it was completely out of his hands.

Whatever was going to be the outcome. He knew he had to deal with it. The next morning came. After a long night that seemed like it would never end.

Which he barely got any rest. The transport bus came, the paddy wagon picked him up along with the other prisoners. Before they board the transport vehicle, Ty and the other arrested people had to stand in front of the police front desk. Then they were hand cuffed and escorted to the back where the transport bus was.

The transport vehicle as known as the paddy wagon, transported the arrested people to central bookings. When they got there, they had to be re-fingered printed all over again. Also, another mugged shot had to be taken again, as well.

During this process, they waited in another jail cell. Ty was just like everybody else, he had to waited ex-number of hours to see the judge. While he sat there in the bull pin. One of the court office clerks called his name.

Ty came to the front of the jail cell bars to speak with the clerk. The clerk asked him a few questions. She asked him was he working or was he in school.

He told her; he was employed. Ty asked her what time it was. Which was odd to her. But she told him the time anyway, because clearly, he was not going anywhere anytime soon. She asked him why he wanted to know what time it was?

He told her, he supposed to been at work an hour ago. She just gave him a weird look after that statement. She asked him was there anybody who could verify who he was. She needed a phone number from him to do that. He gave her his house number.

He told her to ask for Dana. Ty hoped that it would not be that serious. He did have money hidden away in a stash in his place. He had money to pay bills for a period. But he could not support that for a substantial amount of time.

Without him, he knew his family would struggle. Not only financially, but all the above. He was not worried about holding himself down in jail. That was not the problem.

He was more worried that Dana would not be able to support without him. He did not say she cannot do it by herself. But he was concerned with the fact. He really did not want to put that burden on her.

Yes, he still had many connections on the streets. Yes, money was still being made. When you are inside, you do not really know what goes on outside. Contrary to popular belief. Being in jail, you do not have the pull to control everything and everyone outside, to a certain degree.

Ty was a type of man, who did not really trust anybody. That is just the way he was. After waiting and waiting and more waiting, Ty's name was finally called to see the judge.

The judge reviewed his case. The court appointed lawyer was there to defend him. The legal aid lawyer told him; the D.A. offered him a deal.

If he agreed to admit his guilt. He would be released that day. Released with a warning. Ty asked the legal aid lawyer, what was he being charged with. He told him; he was being charged with possession of marijuana.

The evidence showed he had a bag of weed on his persons. The judge asked the legal aid, what Ty wanted to do? He asked Ty. Ty pled guilty over having a bag of weed in his possession. He wanted to get this over with. The judge gave him 6 months' probation of not getting into trouble.

He was released that morning on a R.O. R, just like the court appointed lawyer told him. When Ty inquired about his money, the legal aid lawyer told him not to push it. At first, Ty was going to make a big deal over the lost money.

He realized he got out of this one, with just a warning. Somewhat, a slap on the wrist. So, he took it and ran with it. He had to sign a couple of forms. Then he was ready to leave. He asked about carfare to get home. Since they confiscated his money.

After saying that. They sent him to another room. He was issued carfare to get home. When Ty reached home, it was the middle of the day. First thing first, he threw all the clothes he had on, out in the garbage. Then he took a long hot shower. He went to sleep afterwards.

During his ordeal, he felt like he did not sleep for days. When he woke back up. He wanted to take care of some business. He noticed his car was not parked in front of the apartment building.

Then he remembered, he did tell Dana to pick the car up from the police station. He showered up again. Then he walked to Dana's job. When he got there, the doctor's office was jam packed. He got in touched with Dana. She gave him his car keys. She begins to ask him questions in a crowded clinic.

People looked and wondered and watched, while she talked to him. While everyone was waiting for the doctor. They of course assumed, he was asking questions trying to skip, the already long line. When Dana and Ty looked around, everyone was all in their conversation.

Before she went on with the questioning, she noticed everyone in the waiting area, was waiting for the questions and responses. She looked directly into his eyes, and she told him, that she will be speaking to him later.

She had such a serious look on her face, if looks could kill. Ty would have been a dead man. Tough Ty even felt that vibe she was giving. She handed him the keys with force behind it. He kissed her on her cheek.

She gave a phony smile to the crowd that was watching them in that crowded clinic. Inside, she was upset with him. Ty got into his car and drove off. He went to check out his spots. Plus, on his workers. He had to let them know he was back in town.

On the streets. Some of them shocked. Others was surprised that they did not keep him. The rest of them were only plain ole happy to see him. He collected some money. Then he went back home. Right at that time, he really did not want to be out there on the streets.

He wanted time to himself. He needed to refocus on what was at hand. When Dana got home with the kids. Ty was in the bed under the covers, with the T.V. on. He was watching the television. She told the kids to get started on their homework.

Even the kids knew Dana was not in the mood to be played with. She went into the bedroom and slammed the door behind her.

She started yelling at Ty from the top of her lungs. She even called him a dumb ass! And stupid, for what he did. Then she thought about it. She explained to him, that he was all they got.

And he needs to know and understand that. She gave him a kiss. She told him to think about what she said. Ty remained there laying under the cover. Watching the T.V. but not focus on the television. Laying there thinking about what Dana just said to him. That is what was on his mind.

When she opened the door of the bedroom. The boys ran up to her and asked her was daddy home. She said "Yes!" but she told them, she did not think he wanted to be bothered right now.

Just like any other set of little boys when Dana went to the bathroom. They raced into their parents' bedroom. Lil Ty sat on the side, near the foot of the bed. W.B. hopped in the bed next to his father. He laid on his mother's pillow.

W.B. started touching Ty's forehead, seeing if he had a fever. Like he knew what he was doing. It was just cute, that he was genuinely concerned about his father's well-being.

Ty looked at Lil Ty, while W.B. was playing with his face. Lil Ty asked Ty was he all right. W.B. asked him was he tired. He asked, because he was not used to seeing his father in bed when he got home from school.

Ty felt happy and loved. Ty began to realize, his little men will always have his back, no matter what. They will always love him regardless of the situation. Things like that, meant more than money or materialistic things.

Love is more precious and valuable than anything else in this world. He knew and understood, he had to walk in his own path. The path into which he must lead. Sometimes in life, there is no turning back. You must make the best of it.

Be happy and content with the card's life dealt you. That evening he played with his sons, ate a hot homemade dinner.

He enjoyed a great conversation with his lady. Enjoying the great things, that life had to offer.

Sometimes you must sit down reflect and appreciate things. Think about not having, what you have. To reassure what you really have. It makes you appreciate what you have even more.

Chapter 12

Ty knew, he made a major mistake. He went from being untouchable. To knowing he can be touched. To say the least. Thoughts that he never thought about. Raced through his head.

One day it is all good and the next day total chaos. He knew, he messed up. Whatever happens, happens. At home, whenever Dana asked Ty about that situation, he would just change the subject. Like nothing has happened. Dana was not a dumb person. Far from it.

She knew better than that. With him not answering her questions, just pissed her off. She thought he would of came cleaned by now. She could not understand, why would he keep secrets from her. Before she could think about it. One thing Ty did that was right.

He ensured her that everything is going to be all right. He told her; she did not have to worry about that. Dana knew that he was going through something. She just wanted to help him get through whatever was bothering him. That is what a couple do. To her knowledge.

She still did not have any time to play figure out Ty. She had to look out for her kids. The kids were her main concern. To her, Ty was a grown man. He can take care of himself, if necessary.

Her kids needed to be taken care of. Dana continued her daily routines of dropping the kids off to school. Then she went to work. Dana still went out on some Saturdays with Tanya and her sisters.

After Ty took the boys to the barbershop, to get their haircut. Dana met up with her sisters and her mother at the mall, just like always.

Later, she would drop the boys off at her mothers. Ms. Medina would watch the boys, so Dana could get a break. She knew Dana worked and was a full-time mom. She knew it was not easy. She knew first-hand from her own experiences.

She even told Dana; she should drop the boys off for the whole weekend. So, she did not have to worry about the boys for whole weekend sometimes.

Her family fully supported her. They had her best interest at hand. Ty was happy to be back at work. Even though he wanted more out of life.

Then the half-way decent job he has. He was not complaining, he was happy to at least have a job. Many people could not even say that. At work, he used to be semi-lazy, and carefree, he really did not care about the job too much.

After his ordeal, he became a moderate employee. He started to learn and appreciate what he had. His approach to his job changed. He became a better worker. He did his best at work and cared about being there.

In some cases, he went that extra mile to get the job done. Not only his actions at work. Even his attitude changed. His attitude got much better. Even his bosses took notice of that.

The new changed and improved Ty, they liked it. The supervisors did not question it either. At work, he was the first one there and the last to leave in the evening. He never turns down overtime.

No matter the time it took, or what it consisted of. He did not care, he just wanted to work. He knew that is where he needed to keep his mind on.

Just like his father taught him, when you work hard, only good things come out of it. That is exactly what he wanted to happen.

Lords knows that is what he wanted. On the other hand, the drug operation was doing well. The police officers were not worrying about it. The spot was not hot anymore. Which was better for Ty and his businesses.

Money was good. But with more money, comes more problems. Money comes quick and money goes even quicker. Ty was not taking anything for granted. Instead of spending money. He would save an abundance of money.

Just for rainy days. He already was saving, he realized, he should save even more. He was aware, that he did not know what tomorrow may bring.

On the streets, he made sure, he watched his front and back. Watching himself thoroughly. Always thinking before he made any moves. He knew from day one, that the streets do not love anybody.

Ty knew he was not excluded from that stat. There is no exception to these rules. Ty knew this. Ty took more time out, to spend with his sons. He wanted to enjoy his boys. He took them to football, basketball, baseball games. He took them everywhere.

Dana loved the fact, that he took time out with their kids. She was not saying he did not care before. He was just more into it now. Before you knew it, the ordeal that he went through became a thing of the past. They began to move on. A lot of good days were on the way.

It was all a matter of time. What Ty was doing, Dana could not ask for more. Ty started taking Dana out more often. They began to plan date nights. Taking her to concerts and dinner. Taking walks along the boardwalk. Things she loves to do.

They went on weekend trips, get-a-ways. They were enjoying the good things in life. He told her, she deserved this all and then some. She felt like she was falling in love with Ty all over again. He wanted to treat his queen, like a queen. He made sure they had him and her time.

Ty did not want any time to slip away. He was not taking any time nor anyone for granted. He wanted to show love and time to his family. He realized that is all, that he has. He plain out wanted to show them, how he felt about them.

Precious memories that can last a lifetime. Not only with money. But also, with time. Lil Ty was ecstatic about his father teaching him how to throw and catch a ball.

He taught him how to hit a baseball too. Ty taught Lil Ty how to ride a bike. Not only did he do things with Lil TY. He taught W.B. how to tie his sneakers. Dana was so happy that Ty was acting like the man, she always knew he could be. Dana was happy and in love with the man of her life.

Ty was happy being there for his family. Not only for them, but it also made Ty happy, full of love as well. He felt great, he was able to do these things for his family. What he got out of it, was the feeling of being loved. Time is worth more than money. Even having a good time without spending excessive amounts of money.

Like when him and Dana went to the park, he bought two hot dogs and two sodas. That made the day. He spent little to nothing on it. And the food was just as good as a high priced, 5-star restaurant.

Maybe it was not the food, maybe it had all to do with the power of love. Ty was happy, the boys were happy. Dana was overly joyed with it all. What more could anybody want. They were finally living the way Ty wanted them to live.

Maybe some crooked things got him there. But if you asked him, he would tell you it is worth all of this. Because the way he felt at the time was priceless.

AVAILABLE @AMAZON.COM @BARNESANDNOBLE.COM. @WALMART.COM